Illustrated Girl

Book One in The Chronicles Of Lucitopia

Josephine Angelini

LOS ANGELES

ISBN: 979-8-9878321-2-7

Cover by Bianca Sate

Published by Sungrazer Publishing LLC

For John T. McLeod, my font of dry wit

❧ I ❧

I HAVE FIFTEEN DAYS TO LIVE

Fifteen days. I still can't believe my time is almost up. Three hundred and fifty days have passed since I got myself into this mess, and now I've only got one choice left to make. I can either give up, or I can keep doing what I've been doing for nearly a year, which is trying to find a real boy to kiss me and break this spell.

Not easy to do when you've been turned into an illustration in a book.

The book I live in is LONG. It has many characters, but I'm not the main character. I don't come in until nearly the end. Which is lucky for me because the beginning of this book has all kinds of monsters and stab-happy warriors, and a huge battle against an evil sorcerer. Spoiler alert. He wins. So, yeah, that's the world I live in. The one ruled by an evil sorcerer turned king.

I spend most of my days hiding at the top of a tall

tower because said evil sorcerer king is rattling around out there somewhere in the margins and there aren't a lot of good characters left in this book. Most of the heroes died in the Great Battle between good and evil at Knob Knoll and the rest of the almost-heroes (the ones with enough common sense to run for it when the battle went sideways) are being hunted down. Makes me almost grateful that I can't skip back a bunch of pages and go there. Way too much senseless slaughter for my tastes.

Other characters who have survived up to the point where I come in have told me bits and pieces about what happened, and not kidding here, but I have about a snowball's chance in hell of making it through one week in the majority of this book.

My problem is, all the real boys who read my book *love* the beginning, the middle, and most of the end. Then they stop reading before the final pages. They never make it to the part where I come in. Any eligible boy who might possibly fall madly in love with me when he reads about my imprisonment tends to get angry when the main character, some swashbuckling blockhead named Torvold, gets killed with only fifty pages left to go.

Readers start the book, but so far, every single one of them has stopped reading as soon as Torvold dies. One kid even put the book in the freezer to punish it, which I thought was a little excessive. Twenty-four prospective kissers have read my book in the past three hundred and fifty days, and not one of them has gotten all the way through to the words: THE END. I can't say I blame them. I'm not a fan of books that kill the main characters, either.

Now I've got just fifteen days, and then I'm stuck here. And I will definitely die here. People shoot each other in the *face* with *arrows* here. On a regular basis. They don't even fight first; they just go, "Ho, there! Stop or I'll lose my arrow!" and then they just shoot without waiting to see if the other guy stops.

It's a miracle I've lasted this long. That's not to say that I'm completely incapable of taking care of myself. Since I got trapped here, I've gotten pretty handy with a dagger. Sixteen-going-on-seventeen-year-old virgins are a hot commodity in this book, and I have no intention of being carried off by anyone. But even if I have learned to hold my own, I'm not meant for this type of life. Mostly because of the "commodity" thing that I just mentioned.

In this world women are ranked somewhere above goats, but definitely below horses. I've managed to reduce my reaction to an eye roll every time someone says something dumbfoundingly misogynistic rather than launch into a diatribe, but I've had it. The princess thing is not what I thought it was going to be. Not at all.

I've got to get out of here. I have to go back *lots* of pages, to way before Mother Maybe tricked me, turned me into a character, and stuck me in this book. I have to find a way to get into this story before Torvold dies his heroically lame-brained death. If I can do that, there's bound to be a reader out there who'll fall in love with me and kiss me.

Failing that, at least I might get a pity kiss. I'll take a kiss from anyone. Boy, girl, doesn't matter to me. Lots of girls could be reading this story.

I am not picky. I might even kiss a girl and like it. Who knows? I've never kissed anyone so why limit myself so early in the game?

Someone, please, kiss me.

Still nothing?

sigh

I know you're reading this. It could be you, you know. *You* could be my hero.

crickets

Dang it.

Maybe no one is reading. I can't tell if I'm being read or not. All I hear is gossip in the market about Jinksy the Blind Man who, paradoxically, can only see when a pair of giant eyes are hovering in the sky. The other characters in this book have no idea what that is, but I've always thought that it's a *reader*.

But maybe I'm wrong. Maybe I have no audience, and yet my story continues. My pathetic story of unobserved desperation. At least I know the answer to that question about the tree falling in the woods. It makes a sound, alright, and, if my life is any analogy, it's saying *ohcrapwhyme!*

If you're wondering why I'm not using stronger

language to describe my situation, it's not because I don't want to use every colorful curse word in the book. It's because I can't. The story I'm in is rated middle grade. That means if I couldn't say it in front of a ten-year-old, I can't say it in here. *The Chronicles of Lucitopia* has other stories in it, stories where they can say more than *hang it all* when they stub their toe really hard, but not in my story. Figures I'd pick the one that was suitable for all ages. It's a special kind of torture.

Not exactly what I had in mind when I wished to live in in a world of knights and princesses and magic and... okay, yes, I admit it. Romance. Big, sweeping romance with life-or-death stakes, and a gorgeous boy who'd die for me. You know, real epic fantasy-type stuff, with a steamy romance that makes you swoon when you read about it. I used to do a lot of reading, and a lot of swooning.

I made a wish and I got it, only to find that in the world of Lucitopia, if you walk around with your head in the clouds, someone will chop it off for you.

Today is market day. It's the one day every month that the last few surviving non-evil people of Lucitopia get together to buy, sell, trade, beg, barter, and steal. I know what you're thinking. If someone steals, they're one of the bad guys, right? Heck no. Real bad guys burn villages to the ground and carry off all the women under the age of twenty. Stealing is, like...*nice* here. Almost a compliment, really. If someone tries to take your stuff it's because your stuff is useful, and they probably really need it.

I don't even get upset about it because the coin I use to buy what I need at the market isn't really mine. I found a giant chest full of loot in my tower and I've just been helping myself to it ever since. But I also don't get upset about the perpetual theft because there are a lot of old people in this world. They're all that's left after the Final Battle that killed all the young men, and then after the battle, all the young maiden carrying off stuff. These old people are not as nimble as I am, and if they've mustered up the gumption to do a snatch-and-grab on a loaf of bread that I was stupid enough to leave sticking out of my satchel, I don't try to chase them. They never get more than a dozen paces before they have to stop and wheeze for a bit anyway. I usually let them have it.

If you don't want to get robbed, stay in your tower. That's just common sense.

But I'm okay with a completely non-violent and arthritically impaired mugging today because last market day I heard that Mother Maybe, the old boot who hoodwinked me, is going to be there this time. News of her coming was quite a hullabaloo (I use words like hoodwinked and hullabaloo now to fit in) because it had been rumored that our new sovereign, King Asphodel the Ghastly, had killed her.

King Asphodel has been hunting down a lot of people since the Final Battle at Knob Knoll. It's sort of his thing, actually. Even before he was King Asphodel the Ghastly, back when he was just Asphodel the Evil Sorcerer, he had a penchant for hunting people down. In his tumescent rise to glory, Asphodel killed off all the White Witches, who were the anthropomorphic personifications of the Virtues. He took them out one by one, and thusly clawed his way to the top of the poop-heap that is current Lucitopia.

Compassion was the first to go because, by nature, she was a giant sucker, quickly followed by Humility, who apologized during her own murder. Next went Cleanliness who was too busy mopping up the blood spilled by Compassion and Humility to protect herself, and then Punctuality who showed up right on time for her own funeral.

After that, Lucitopia went to hell in a handbasket. There isn't even a record of when and how each of the remaining White Witches was bumped off. Probably because Vigilance was killed before she could write it down.

That's the world that I'm stuck in. Do you know what a knight is without Virtue? Meat in a tin can. About as appealing as cat food.

It's so stinky here without Cleanliness, and everyone's late now that Punctuality's dead. I hate BO, I hate it when people don't show up on time, and I can't take it anymore. I feel like I'm always waiting around for smelly people. I'm getting out while I still can, even if it kills me. So with this decision made, I've packed a few things in my satchel just in case I'm able to set out from the market immediately. Of course, this is *if* I can get Mother Maybe to put me in the story earlier.

I double-check my pack because you can never be too prepared. I've got a bedroll, flint, and spare daggers; replacements for the ones I keep in my bodice, my garters, my sleeves. Oh, and in my boots. I've got some animal traps, so I can feed myself. I've got a waterskin, and salt. I never understood how important salt was until I got here. Ever try to eat squirrel with no seasoning? If you haven't, don't. I've also got a few spells in here in case everything goes bunk.

I'm as prepared as I can get, I guess. Here I go, out of my nice, safe tower with all its salt, provisions, and easily defensible positioning. I'm stalling. I know. It just *really* sucks out there. Okay. Here I go. One, two, three...

I heave my collection of skirts and corsets over the ledge and use the braid of crazy long hair left here by the former inhabitant (I assume she made it out okay) to lower myself down. Now I just have to navigate through the magical minefield around my tower. The minefield is harder to get through going *out* than coming *in*. I have a feeling the former owner of the hair was not exactly a willing participant in her tower dwelling.

Magical spells come in all shapes and sizes, as you'd imagine, but they have a few basic design parameters in common. Most of them have a small radius of influence, and they only work a few times. Think of spells as semi-reusable land mines (if you step on one) or grenades (if you cast one). They are also one-hundred-percent illusion.

Magic doesn't actually change anything. It only tricks your brain into believing something has happened. That being said, if your brain thinks a poisonous monster just bit your arm off, it's still going to hurt. A lot. The spell will go away on its own eventually, but in the meantime, you will not be able to see, use, or feel that arm. Except for the excruciating agony that you would expect from having your arm bit off.

Of course, none of what I just said applies to really strong spells cast by great sorcerers. Those *can* change the world around them. Luckily, that kind of magic is extremely rare and difficult to do. Even a great sorcerer can only pull off a handful of such spells in a lifetime because they kind of almost kill the sorcerer to do them.

But illusion messes with your head enough, in my opinion. On my first foray out of the tower, way back when I still believed in things like Kindness (dead) and Fairness (*way* dead), I stumbled over an ax-in-the-face spell. That was a very bad day. After a few hours of writhing around on the ground in blinding pain, I concluded that it couldn't be real. There was no way I could survive an ax in my face for longer than about a millisecond. From that point on, I understood how magic worked in this stupid book and now if something happens to me and it seems impossible, I call baloney and ignore it until it goes away.

Still, I place my boots carefully as I work my way across

the open ground surrounding my tower and toward the outer stone wall circling the hold.

I know there's a bugs-crawling-all-over you spell at the gate between the outer stone wall and the path, thanks to some bandits who unsuccessfully tried to carry me off. I never go through the front gate. Instead, I jump the wall to the right of it, put my skirts over my head to slog through some sludge, which I assume was some kind of moat at one time, scramble up the other bank, and then haul myself up onto the path.

I'm damp, muddy, and cranky by the time I start my six-mile hike to the market.

Another lovely day dawns in Lucitopia.

2

MOTHER MAYBE IS A MEAN OL' @ITCH

They call it a market, but really, it's more like a carnival. Except pretty much everyone looks like a skeevy carnie, even the people who come here to buy stuff.

There are acrobats, artisans, games of chance, clowns who are utterly terrifying, and jugglers. There are those dudes on stilts, strong men, and bearded ladies. There are food stands and magical animal auctions (up for sale today: two angry Brownies dressed like pixies, and one very confused goose that probably does not lay golden eggs) and of course, there's a greased warthog catching contest. I mean, who can pass up the chance to try and grab a greased warthog?

Hawkers tell me I'd be getting the opportunity of a lifetime—*three beans could grow you a palace in the sky*—as I walk by. The air smells like fried dough and cotton candy when I get a lucky twist in the breeze, and like foot and armpit when I don't. There's a lot of energy and glitter, but like any carnival that isn't part of an entertainment park owned by a massive corporation, there is also the dinginess of poverty creeping up all the brightly striped tents and banners like mold. Actually, I think most of it is mold.

Harmless spells create the illusion of pomp and circumstance. Unicorns paw at the ground in front of gilded temples, but turn the corner and you can see in one glimpse out of a thousand, that they're really just some sway-backed nags in front of a tattered tent. Fireworks burst endlessly in the sky with no smoke or boom. Everything that is beautiful is magic, and magic is nothing but illusion.

And there aren't any kids. That's one of the weirdest things about Lucitopia. No babies, no children. I'm the youngest person here by far.

Don't get me wrong, I'm not baby-crazy or anything. I mean, I *like* babies. I used to babysit on the weekends for my neighbors, and they had this little boy who was kind of great because he used to laugh every time I blew raspberries on his cheek and he only cried when he had a wet diaper. His parents would leave for date night, we'd play ten minutes of peek-a-boo, I'd give him a bottle, a bath, and that kid was out like a light while I ate Doritos and read books on my phone until the 'rents came home at midnight. I was basically getting paid to do what I would be doing on a Saturday night anyway, but without having to listen to my parents arguing in the background. Easy money.

I know babies can be really annoying. Except when there aren't any. Just try to picture it. You look around and realize that you're at a carnival, but there's no one laughing or screaming because they're so happy they can't keep it in anymore. No one is jumping up and down in front of the glass blower because a person used fire to melt glass into syrup that became a dragon. There isn't even anyone to run screaming from the terrifying clowns. That's when you realize that kids are annoying, yes, but they are also *supposed* to be there. And there aren't any here.

Lucitopia is dying.

Being the youngest person by an average of six decades does not mean that I don't get harassed, by the way. Not in Lucitopia. Once, this dusty mummy of a dude tried to reverse whistle at me—you know, that type of whistle where they pretend you're so hot that they got burned just looking at you and they suck the air *in* through their teeth? Yeah, well, while he was sucking in, his last tooth came out and he choked on it. I had to give him the Heimlich. Afterward, he asked me to marry him, which I thought was decent of him, considering the unintentional intimacy of the maneuver.

"Buying or selling?" a thousand-year-old creep asks, right on cue. "Please tell me you're selling."

"Stow it, Dracula, or I'll plunk a stake in your heart," I tell him.

I feign a British accent to fit in. Everyone here has one. Don't know why, exactly, except that British accents are pretty much required in these kinds of vaguely medieval magical epic fantasy stories. If you think about it, how ridiculous would a movie about knights and sorcerers be if everyone had a Brooklyn accent?

"Dracula" laughs so hard he sends himself into a coughing fit. He has no idea what I'm talking about, of course. There is no Dracula in Lucitopia, I don't think. He's just having a laugh because I gave him some sass.

At this point, the geezers at the market just hassle me to see what I'll say to them. We all sort of know each other by now, but only in a side-eyes sort of way. I keep my hand on the dagger in my belt as I pass him, just in case, and quash a smile.

I shake my head at someone who's paying a little too much attention to my satchel, and when he abruptly abandons his attempted robbery, I make my way down Fortune Alley, where all the old con ladies flock together like a murder of crows.

"Come for your fortune, dearie?" cackles a fat woman with a sequined shawl, dyed black hair, and mawkishly painted-on lips.

"That'd be stupid," I say bluntly. "There is no future here."

She closes her mouth with a snap. Then she adjusts her

shawl and sniffs, like she's too good for me. Her eyes dart up to the golden circlet around my head.

"Why come down Fortune Alley then, princess?" she asks. "You won't find any real boys to kiss you here."

Does she know? I have to be careful because one of the rules of being in Lucitopia is that I can't let on to anyone that I'm from another world, or I'm stuck here forever. But some of the characters here, like Mother Maybe, know we're inside a storybook. If this lady already knows, she might be able to help me get out.

"You know how I have to be kissed by a real boy to get out of here?" I hazard.

"The Great Griselda sees all and knows all," she intones, totally not answering my question.

"How fortuitous." I get in her face. "Because I need to find Mother Maybe."

"I know all, for a *price*," Griselda corrects.

"Yeah." I chuckle, pulling out my dagger. "But I bet you'll tell all to save your life." Her face goes blank. She's not so sure she likes where this is headed anymore. "Didn't see *that* coming, did you?"

I'm being a jerk, but so is she. Why can't anyone here just give me directions or help me find someone or not try and take me for every cent if I ask them for the frigging time of day? Everyone in Lucitopia is a jerk, and I hate having to be one in return.

And let me be clear about something. I'm not going to hurt her. But here in Lucitopia if you haul out your purse like a gap-toothed bumpkin and say *how much* every time someone tells you *it's going to cost you,* they never give you want you want. They just keep finding new and interesting ways to take your money while they lead you on a merry jaunt across this rat-infested hell. I don't know if she's in on the whole Lucitopia thing or not, but quite frankly I don't have the time to find out.

"Just take me to Mother Maybe," I tell her, shrugging tiredly. "If you do, I'll give you enough money to buy ten sparkly shawls. Okay?"

She nods hastily, never taking her eyes off my dagger. I do sort of have a reputation for being good with a dagger.

To be honest, in the beginning, I got lucky. Couple of bandits, a few well-thrown knives that by some miracle hit a few tender bits, and word got around. Then I practiced. A lot. I don't know if I could live up to the reputation I've got now, but like I said. Bunch of old people. When the majority of my opponents would sooner throw their backs out than throw a dagger, I probably don't have to be all that good to be considered amazing.

"This way," Griselda says with far less cackle in her voice than previously.

As she walks in front of me, I notice the rounding in her back eases away and the fat in her middle stretches out as she stands up taller. She is, in fact, neither short nor fat. Nor is she all that old. Maybe in her fifties? Not young, but certainly not old and feeble. In fact, she looks quite hale.

Griselda leads me down a few switchback alleys behind the main drag. The tents here are made of less garish material, but they're cleaner and they reek less. She comes to a small canvas tent that's a basic olive-green color and stops at the opening flap.

"I'm not saying she'll help you," Griselda says. She suddenly has a beautiful voice, and not a cackle to be found. "But she's been waiting for you. Too long, I think."

I don't know what to say. This Griselda is much different from the Great Griselda who tried to swindle me. She seems almost—*stately* is the only word that comes to mind.

I take a step. I don't know why I'm hesitating. I shake myself and reach for my purse. A deal's a deal. Griselda holds up a hand.

"Please," she says, refusing to take my money. "Mother Maybe is waiting." She holds the tent flap open for me and follows me in.

"She's here," Griselda calls out.

"Well, well, well," says a sighing voice.

Mother Maybe looks the same as she did at the swap meet on Fairfax and Santa Monica. Like a tatty Stevie Nicks. She wears fringed, dreamy boho clothes that are a little worse for wear. She has thick, long, curly blonde hair, an upturned nose, and just enough of a figure left to let you know she was smoking hot about twenty years ago. She comes out from behind a partition that runs the length of the tent carrying tea in a mug that says *unicorns are boneheads* in worn words on the side of it.

She gives me a look that's normally accompanied by a tisking sound, and then goes back to stirring her tea. "Finally done waiting for Prince Charming to come and save you?"

I hate it when people say *well, well, well*. I also hate it when they trap me in dangerous fairy tales. I should give her a piece of my mind. Too bad I'm still hung up on that last thing she said about waiting to be saved.

"What do you even mean by that? You're the one—you *told* me I had to get someone to kiss me!" I stammer.

"And you thought the best way to go about that was to climb a tower and sit on your butt?" She perches a fist on her hip. "No wonder everyone stops reading you. You're passive. No one likes a passive character."

"The king sent me to that tower!" I think anyway. I was in the tower when I got to Lucitopia, and I'm pretty sure my dad had sent me there at the beginning of the book, which we've already established I did *not* read.

"But you didn't have to stay there," Mother Maybe countered infuriatingly.

"I was trying to not get killed!"

She smirks at me. "And you think trying not to get killed is going to win you a huge fan base, do you?"

My mouth is hanging open. I shut it and try to look outraged. "You never told me it was going to be like this."

She makes a face like she knows *I* know I'm lying. "You

came to my table and started digging through my books. I asked you what you liked to read." She gestures around her. "Ta-da!"

"You made me get this stupid book, and by the way, you are a *terrible* used book saleswoman because I specifically said that I liked a strong romance in my Arthurian fantasy. Where's the romance!?" I put a fist on my hip to match hers, but it's really just a watered-down version of hers. Fists on hips only work if you've got some meat there to really land it. I recover and get back to picking the bone I have with her. "Plus, I never thought it would be real."

She smiles at me. "But you hoped with all of your heart that it would be. I told you to be careful, that you couldn't take it back, and you went right ahead and said the words."

I don't have an answer for her because she's right. Crap, I think I might cry.

"I misjudged you, that's true," she admits, nodding sadly. "I thought you could be the one."

"Oh. Great. *You're* disappointed in *me* now?" I retort. Good old sarcasm. Saving me from yet another emotional moment. "I stayed alive. I didn't want to die like a—a..."

"Like a hero," she finishes for me.

"I'm from *Fresno*. There are no heroes in Fresno!"

She turns away from me, heading for the partition. She's going to leave. She's going to leave and I'm going to be stuck in miserable Lucitopia forever.

"Wait!" I plead. "You have to help me."

"I don't know what you think I can do for you. You had a shot, and you blew it. Everyone stops reading when you go and hide."

"Then send me back to the middle of the book, where there are still people reading," I whisper. "Send me back before the battle on Knob Knoll. Please. I still have fifteen days."

"Fourteen and a half," she corrects sternly.

"Better than nothing."

She smiles. "That's the spirit."

Then she looks me over. She's got green eyes. That kind of green that can be mistaken for blue unless you're looking right into them. And she smells like patchouli, but not in a head-shop way. She smells nice, actually. And she's got great skin. Lucitopia's one perk. I haven't had a pimple since I got here, but in the real world, I have a face full of acne. Too bad I haven't been able to enjoy my newly awesome complexion because I've been too busy avoiding rape and pillage.

Mother Maybe turns to Griselda. "What do you think?" she asks her.

Griselda narrows her eyes, considering. "She's got some skills now, but skipping back that far?" She shakes her head.

Mother Maybe smiles at her. "You wouldn't be you if you weren't cautious," she says, and then she turns to me. "Okay. I'll send you back, but on one condition."

I roll my eyes. "Anything. And, yes, please, give me a

condition or a clue or something because I have no idea what the heck you want from me."

Mother Maybe pushes back a panel of the partition and gestures for me to go behind it. "No more waiting around to be saved. Make your life the story you'd want to read."

3

TORVOLD THE BOLD IS TOTALLY HOT

I've done the shift through time, space, and most likely reality itself once before to get to Lucitopia, but it's still really disorienting.

Being instantaneously *placed* somewhere and somewhen else is a complete who's-your-daddy of all your senses. There's a feeling of apprehension, like a giant butterfly in your stomach. Except not a good butterfly. A barfy one. Everything looks wavy around the edges, but it's more than a visual change. There's a temperature shift, too, and the smells in the air are completely different. Oh, and just a suggestion: if you're walking, *stop*.

Suddenly blinded by bright sunlight, I take a step and put my foot down on a loose rock. I think I recover for a second, only to realize that, no, I do not have my balance yet, because I'm not standing on the flat bottom of a tent anymore, but on a slope. Then, while I'm waving my arms about and doing some kind of goofy hip thrust that probably looks a lot like the Pee-Wee Herman dance, I pitch headlong into a gurgling stream, scraping the palms of my hands on the gravel at the bottom and soaking myself with cold mountain meltwater.

"Ho, there!" calls a young man's voice.

And apparently, I'm about to get shot in the face with an arrow. Great.

"Are you injured?" He sounds worried. About my well-being. That's new.

I must have moved to a part of the book where Kindness hasn't gotten the ax yet.

"No," I say, switching to my fake British accent. My hair is plastered over my eyes. I inch out of the river on my hands and knees rather than attempt to stand up while still partially blinded.

"Stay where you are, milady. I will cross the river and assist you," he says. I hear splashing and clanking coming toward me as I crawl. That clanking is probably armor. Hopefully, he's a knight and not a bandit. Kindness is probably still around, but this is Lucitopia, after all. He could be a *kind* bandit.

"What horrible spell has abandoned you in such a state in the Forest of Woe? Was it Asphodel—curse his name!"

Passionate fellow. And that British accent he's got makes everything sound more poetic.

"Ah. No. And you don't have to—" I say, but he's already lifting me up and carrying me.

I'd protest, but he moves fast. Before I have much chance to push myself away from his chainmail-covered chest, he places me down on a convenient hillock of grass. I throw my bedraggled hair off my face. It takes a few tries to get enough hair out of my face to see because the stupid circlet around my head keeps getting in the way. And I've got a ton of smooth, wavy, auburn hair. It's so long I can sit on it. Another perk, courtesy of Lucitopia. In the real world, my head is covered in something that looks suspiciously like rusty brown yeti fur. It's dull, frizzy, and won't grow much past my shoulders.

He looks stunned. "Princess Pleasant?" he says. Then he moves back and, distressingly, goes down on one knee in front of me. "What are you doing out here in the wild? You should be safe in your tower!"

"No more towers," I say, stopping him right there. "I'm out in the wild because—"

Why am I out here in the wild? What could my character, the only child of the true king, be doing running around the dreaded Forest of Woe? I have no idea. I take my pack off my shoulder and start going through it, like I'm making sure nothing important is damaged, to give myself a chance to think.

In the small part of the book I had time to read before I said the spell and got myself stuck in here, Princess Pleasant is hidden away because Asphodel the Ghastly (at this point in the story he's still Asphodel the Evil Sorcerer) has been demanding her hand in marriage so that he can be the next king, and her father won't allow it, because no one wants an evil sorcerer in the family. Or as a future king.

That's the story as it is written. Princess Pleasant doesn't even have any dialogue in the book, as far as I know. There's just an illustration of her. She's really pretty, and she's wearing a great dress and a golden circlet on her head, and I loved the illustration as soon as I saw it. She was like that Waterhouse painting of the Lady of Shalott, but less horsy-faced. She had great skin, great hair, and a killer wardrobe, but that's about all there is in the book about Princess Pleasant. She isn't even a full character, like Torvold is. She's just an illustration. Like an idiot, I thought that being pretty and having great clothes would make my life perfect. Dead wrong about that, by the way.

I'm going to have to think up a darn good reason for me to be wandering around a monster-infested forest, or this knight is going to drag me back to some dumb tower, and I know how that ends for me. I want to get out of here, and the only instruction Mother Maybe gave me was to make my story the one I'd want to read.

So, what would I want to read?

"I'm on an important quest...er...from my father... um...the king." That didn't sound wishy-washy at all, right? "I need your help, brave knight."

He bows even lower, which shouldn't be possible in chain mail, but he's quite flexible, apparently.

"And I, Sir Torvold the Bold, will aid you in your quest, my princess," he swears. He looks up at me.

Wow. He's really good-looking, but he's not cute. He's no baby face, even though I can tell he's young, probably my age, maybe a year or two older. He's got brown hair, brown eyes, and a cleft chin. It's very hero-esque, that cleft. Not something I would personally choose if I had written this book, but it works. He's got the whole sharp cheekbones and granite jaw thing going, and the cleft really pulls it all together. I bet he wasn't one of those angelic-looking little boys who people went goo-goo over, but you can tell he's growing into himself. And several other people, from the size of him. He's *huge*. Not in a freaky knuckle-dragging way, but tall and muscular and just, wow.

While I'm staring, something warm, soft, and hairy blows hot air down my neck. I'm doing the Pee-Wee Herman again trying to get away from it and headed back into the river for another dunking, but Torvold catches me and swings me up in his arms. This guy is nimble.

"Fear not, my princess," Sir Torvold says with a smile and a dimple. "That is my trusty steed, Thunder. Come, do your duty to her Highness, Thunder."

Sir Torvold places me back on my feet for the second time while I hold out my hand for the horse to sniff. I don't have a lot of experience with horses, but they can't be too different from dogs, can they? He nudges my hand and I scratch him under the chin.

Thunder is one of those horses with the furry hooves that I've only ever seen pulling giant sleighs in beer commercials during football games, except he's all white. His face is bigger than my torso. He nods his head, tossing his long, silky mane, and paws the ground with a hoof. Almost like he's bowing, strangely enough.

"A-hem," a small voice says from somewhere in the back. Since horse's butts can't speak, not even here in Lucitopia, I assume there's someone else with us.

"Ah! And that's my trusty squire, Jackanet the Tidy," Torvold says heartily.

Jackanet comes out from behind Thunder, twisting his cap in his hands. He gives me a very shaky bow and then stands again, still clutching his cap in his filthy hands. His hose is wrinkled and slipping down on his scrawny legs, giving him baggy ankles. There are several gravy stains on his jerkin and his cape is covered in shed horsehair.

Jackanet the Tidy does not live up to the hype. I would accuse Sir Torvold of sarcasm, but I don't think he knows what that is.

"Pleased to meet you?" Jackanet says uncertainly, probably because I'm still staring at him, trying to figure out if they're both just messing with me or not. "Would you like me to help you...you know...tidy up?" he asks me.

"Oh, no," I say too loudly. I'm a hot mess right now, but he'd definitely make it worse. And probably give me pinkeye. "Modesty forbids it," I say, playing the girl card.

"Well, I should go and find the...you know..." Jackanet says, sidling away from us with Thunder.

"Sorry, the what?" Sir Torvold says.

"The er-tues that we're er-tecting," he grumbles incoherently, glaring at Torvold.

Torvold scrunches up his face. "Have you got something in your throat, Jackanet?"

The squire gives his master a blank look followed by an eye roll, and then he simply walks away from us, taking the horse with him.

"And now, my princess, tell me your quest so I might aid you in it," Sir Torvold says, not missing a beat in his up-beatness.

My quest. My quest? My quest, quest, questidty quest-quest. Not many q words are there? Rats. I don't have a quest. I must deflect.

"How remiss of me! What is *your* quest, brave knight?"

"I have been given the sacred task of protecting Virtue itself. I must find and protect every White Witch still alive," he replies gravely.

Now that's a quest. But I wouldn't go around announcing that if I were him. This is Lucitopia. Nobody tells anyone what they want unless they want that other person to try to take it away from them. Or make them pay double for it.

But that's *my* Lucitopia, the one with no Virtue. I look at Torvold and realize that he is from another place entirely, even if it does have the exact same name. And then I mentally translate what his squire was mumbling about.

"Oh! Is that what Squire Jackanet left to seek? Have you lost your Virtues?" I ask. Torvold blushes deeply and I backpedal. "Obviously, good sir, you are virtuous to the core; I only meant—"

"Yes, yes," he says, nodding a little too vigorously. "They are not *my* virtue, I've still got that, though I hope I have their Virtues in me as well." He seems to realize that this is getting worse by the second. "I am the guardian of two White Witches. There. That's what I'll call them from now on. White Witches."

"Much easier," I agree. I'm nervous. I don't know why. He basically just told me he was a big, hot virgin.

"But enough about my quest. Tell me yours, my princess."

He's on a quest to find and protect all that is good in the world. I don't have anything that comes close to that. I'm going to have to vamp until I come up with something.

"My quest is so unexpected...and secret...and...and... clandestine that my father could trust none with it but me," I say, waving one arm and clutching my bosom with the other.

I'll give him a little of the old razzle dazzle until I can come up with a really good quest. No—a *great* quest. One that would definitely make tons of guys desperate to keep reading until they fall in love with me. Or girls. Still not picky, because that's how these stories go, right? I'm convinced through the whole thing that I'm supposed to kiss a guy, but it turns out it's a girl in the end. Well, I'm not getting hung up on that, I can tell you. I'd totally kiss a girl. Just saying, if any girls are reading this and want to give it a go, I am *so* game.

Still nothing, huh?

"Forgive me, Princess, but you seem distracted," Torvold interjects politely.

"Just contemplating the onerous task I have been given, kind sir," I reply. Onerous? I've got to stop using adjectives or I'm going to paint myself into a corner. Now I've got to come up with an *onerous* quest. Great.

His big brown eyes round with empathy. Holy *gawd*. They actually glimmer. A saintly beam of light has fallen through the trees, hit his face at just the right angle, and made his eyes freaking glimmer. These romance books. They'll be the death of me.

"Share your burden with me. I will help you shoulder it," he says in his deep, soft voice.

Wow. I just stare at him like a nitwit.

"How is your father?" he asks when I don't answer.

"Not well," I reply, thinking of my own father and too stunned by Sir Sexy to put my cosplay filter on.

But I get lucky. Sir Torvold is nodding sadly. "I'd heard. He's been very ill for quite some time now."

"We all hope for his recovery," I say politely.

He looks uncertain, like he is about to say something,

and then he changes his mind. He smiles winningly. "And now, princess," he says, "what brings you here to the Forest of Woe?"

"Monster," I say, pointing.

Because there is a giant lion-lizard-eagle monster coming up behind him.

4
DO YOU LIKE YOUR EGGS SCRAMBLED?

Here's how I know it's a real monster and not just a spell.

One: this is the Forest of Woe, which is known for its monsters and not its spells. Two: spells tend to hit you right away, not stand there yelling at you for a while. If this monster was a spell, I'd both see it and be getting gnawed on by it at the same time. And three: Torvold sees it, too.

Casting a spell on more than one person is really difficult. Not impossible, but difficult. If a sorcerer was going to spend the life force necessary to cast a spell on more than one person, said sorcerer wouldn't just drop it in a forest that had perfectly real monsters of its own.

This monster is completely real. And completely terrifying.

I'm heading back into the river for a third time, but Torvold catches me yet again. He pulls out his sword with one hand and hoists me over one of his shoulders with the other.

"Fear not, my princess," he shouts as he runs into the rushing water, "these types of beasts loathe water."

I push against Torvold's back so I can prop myself up and see behind us while he runs. The view isn't good.

"Yes, well, this one can fly," I shout over the sound of the river.

The lion-lizard-eagle flaps its great wings twice and it's over the river and landing on the far bank before I'm done warning Torvold. The monster starts striding back and forth on the riverbank, waiting for dinner to be done washing itself, and get in his belly.

Torvold switches gears quickly. He stops where he is, wades to about mid-river, finds a rock, and puts me on it.

"Fear not—" Torvold begins, but I cut him off.

"You've got to stop saying that. Fear is an entirely appropriate sentiment, given the situation."

He grins at me. Hello, dimple. Nice to know your owner has a sense of humor.

"Stay here. I'll go kill it," he says simply. He brandishes his sword once and charges through the water as if he were on flat ground. I would be eating gravel right now if I tried that.

Torvold scrambles for the bank, but here he's at a serious disadvantage. He's got to fight the thing uphill across broken ground. Not to mention the fact that the monster is about fifteen feet tall and nearly three times as long.

I see him lose his footing and think, *well that was nice while it lasted,* and then Torvold feints to the side on his actually perfectly solid footing as the monster dips his head down to snap him up. Torvold swings his sword up and around and nearly chops the lion head off. Unfortunately, the mane is probably two feet thick and all that gets cut off is a hank of fur.

Torvold rolls easily up onto the bank next to the monster as it rears back, enraged. He crouches down into a fighting stance, rushes in, but then thinks better of it when the reptilian tail swings around and practically knocks him down. Torvold tries another approach only to find flashing talons almost piercing his chest.

The knight and the monster start circling each other, sizing each other up.

"I'll lead him away. You cross back to the other side and find Jackanet. If I do not return, good luck on your quest, princess," Torvold yells to me, never taking his eyes off the beast.

Torvold starts to back up the far bank to lead the beast away, but as he does so, the long tail that is now facing me shoots out. I try to jump into the river as soon as I see what old anaconda-rear is about, but it catches me in midair. The tail coils around my waist so tightly I feel like I'm going to puke.

There is suddenly a lot more noise. I can hear Sir

Torvold shouting to me, the flapping of wings, and the ringing of a sword against tough scales. The lion's head of the monster starts roaring in pain, but the tail keeps coiling me in. Torvold is fighting like crazy up there as he tries to save me, but in the meantime, I'm rolled up like a burrito underneath this monster's poop shoot.

It is *pungent* down here. And there's something soft and fuzzy resting on my forehead. I don't want to think about what it is because, just based on the little I know about general anatomy, I'm pretty sure it's gotta be his boy bits. Gross.

My arms are squeezed close enough together that I can just barely graze the hilt of one of the blades that I've got tucked up my left sleeve with my right fingertips. I inch the blade out and nick myself pretty good as I spin it around, but I do finally manage to get the hilt held solidly in my right fist. Then I bring it around sharply and cut into a coil of monster muscle.

That loosens his grip enough that I can yank my arms out, but the blade stays stuck inside of Mr. Stinky. My other blades are in my bodice, garters, and my boots, and as such they are inaccessible right now. I get an idea. It's the definition of low blow, but this is life or death, here. I grab ahold of the soft and fuzzy thing resting on my forehead and give it a squeeze.

The monster makes a yelping sound that's legitimately pathetic. He tries to drop me and fly away, but I don't let go of him. I'm too terrified that he'll slash me with the talons on his hind legs as I fall past them. Not to mention the fact that I could break a leg in a bad landing. There's no emergency room in Lucitopia. You break a leg here and you'll have a limp for the rest of your life.

The monster's flapping his wings, trying to get airborne, and I'm swinging from his tenders like a baller hanging from the rim, still twisting and grinding whatever he's got in there like I'm wringing out a pair of wet jeans. Finally, the monster drops back down to earth and keels over.

Torvold vaults onto the monster's belly and slashes it open with a swing that would have every golfer in my world drooling. The beast makes a screeching sound. I decide it's safe to let go and I roll off to the side as Torvold searches under the opened scales for the heart. When he finds it, he drives his blade home, putting the poor creature out of his misery.

Torvold jumps down next to me. "You're bleeding," he says urgently.

He tries to gather me up in his arms again, but at this point, I think I've spent more time being carried around by him than on my own two feet.

"I need no assistance, brave knight, no more than you've supplied by killing this hideous beast that is," I say, holding up a hand to stop him. He looks dismayed and I realize my hand is covered in blood.

"Your hand," he says, unbuckling his chain mail at the shoulder. Underneath is a white linen shirt.

"Tis but a scratch," I protest, but he's already taking off his shirt. I stop talking and just let it happen.

Wow. I never realized how mesmerizing muscles could be. I mean, I've always liked them, but Torvold's are hypnotic. He's not puffed up or anything, but everything flows from his broad chest and shoulders, down his rippling six-pack, to trim hips, in such a harmonious way. Even his back is carved out of thick, curved muscle and his skin is so smooth. I wonder if he shaves—no, that's silly. Guys here don't shave their bodies.

Torvold is just about to start ripping up his shirt to make bandages for my hand when we hear Thunder whinny.

"That was horrible!" Jackanet shouts. He's leading Thunder across the river. On the stallion's back are two barefooted women in white dresses.

Torvold stands and bows to them, and then puts on his shirt. Unfortunately.

"Good. You're here," Torvold says hurriedly as Jackanet arrives on our side of the bank. "I need bandages." He looks Jackanet over. "What's wrong with you? You're as pale as a sheet."

"I've never seen an animal so horribly abused," Jackanet says as he digs in the horse's saddle bags.

"What are you talking about? You've seen me slay dozens of monsters," Torvold replies as he takes some cloths from his squire.

"Not you—her! Did you see how she was swinging from that poor chimera-griff's b—?"

"Jackanet," Torvold scolds, as he wraps my hand. "Language."

"But it's true!" Jackanet continues pointing at me. "She was ringing his bells like there was a village on fire!"

Torvold is blushing and angry and sputtering, and I figure the best way to handle it is to ignore it.

"I have no idea what you're talking about, good squire," I say. "But Sir Torvold was quite the hero this afternoon. He saved me from being carried off by that chimera-griff."

"I can't take all the praise. You fought bravely, too, princess," Torvold insists. I can feel my cheeks heat up at the compliment. But princesses aren't supposed to do things like swing from giant scrotums.

"She's the one who did him in," Jackanet reiterates.

"I was merely holding on for dear life until Sir Torvold could come to my rescue," I say. That sounded princess-y.

Jackanet gives me a disbelieving look, followed by a wary one, like he's deciding to keep his eye on me.

As Torvold finishes with my bandages, Jackanet turns to help the two women down from Thunder's back.

"Princess Pleasant, this is the White Witch Fortitude." Torvold gestures to a stout little woman, maybe in her mid-thirties, with big brown eyes and a long shiny black braid. Her caramel-colored face is round and jolly, yet there is something about her eyes that says she's not as soft on the inside as she is on the outside.

I curtsey to her, "Your Grace," I say.

"No, no. Just call me Tudie, dear. I don't stand on ceremony," she says with a crisp nod.

I smile at her while Torvold directs me to the other White Witch. "And this is Dexterity," he informs me.

I'm momentarily thrown while I have a quick mental debate as to whether or not dexterity could be considered a virtue, but I recover fast and give her a semi-decent curtsey.

"Call me Dex," Dexterity tells me. She has an open, earnest smile. I smile back at her, deciding immediately that I like her.

Dexterity is in her late twenties, and she wears her blonde hair cropped close across the back and around the ears, but with a grown-out mop left on top. She's got long features and lanky limbs. She moves in a loose way, like she's built out of rubber bands. Standing next to short and stout Fortitude, they look like a vaudeville comedy act.

"I'm honored," I tell them, and I'm happy to note that I'm telling the truth. "You may call me—" and here I pause for a moment.

I've always hated the name Princess Pleasant. The writer really phoned it in on that one, but I can't think of a snazzy way to shorten it. *Plez* doesn't exactly roll off the tongue.

"Don't trouble yourself, dearie," Tudie says, waving it

away. "We'll come up with something to call you as we travel apace together, to be sure."

"Come, let us move away from this gory sight," Sir Torvold says considerately. "We will sup together, and the princess can tell us all about her perilous quest."

Drat. I'd rather fight another monster. The party starts to move upstream from the dead chimera-griff, but I hang back.

"I left my...er...pack back there," I say.

Jackanet unhooks my pack from the pommel of Thunder's saddle and passes it to me. "You left it on the other side of the river."

"Right! Many thanks, trusty squire, for retrieving it for me," I say while I put my pack back over my shoulder. "I meant something else I dropped in the fight."

I run back and hastily pull my knife out of poor Mr. Stinky. He was just doing what monsters do. I give him a little pet and whisper, "Sorry," as I clean my blade hastily in the grass. As I'm sliding the blade back into my arm sheath, I catch Jackanet watching me. He hustles off as soon as we make eye contact.

I join the group again and there's a little argument about who is going to ride on Thunder. Everyone insists that I ride because I'm injured, but mostly because I'm a princess, I suspect. I dissent, but I can't really wiggle out of it, though I don't feel right about making two Virtues walk.

We travel upstream until we find a good spot to camp.

I'm thinking about what my quest should be the whole way, but I can't come up with anything both believable and heroic.

"This looks like a favorable place to pass the night," Torvold declares. The spot he's picked is close to the river-bank, but far enough away to be dry. There's a lovely shade tree to sleep under. I look up into the branches to make sure there are no nests above us. I don't want to get pooped on in the middle of the night. And, yes, it has happened to me before.

While I'm looking up into the branches for any possible late-night bombardiers, I feel Torvold's huge, warm hands wrap around my waist. I stiffen with surprise, but he's already sliding me out of the saddle and setting me down on the ground between him and Thunder.

We are awfully close together. I stare at his chest for a moment, thinking about what's under all that chain mail before I look up at him. Another beam of light is filtering down through the leaves and landing perfectly on his head like a halo. The writer must have spent a lot of time describing the light around Torvold, although I bet this guy would look good in the dark. Not that you can see anything in the dark. Why am I thinking about being in the dark with Torvold?

"I have to unsaddle Thunder," he tells me.

"Oh, right," I say, hastily stepping aside when I realize he's been waiting for me to move. I resist the urge to smack myself on the forehead and nonchalantly go over to the White Witches like I didn't just make a fool of myself.

Dex pulls out a pocket knife and some flint. She spins the little blade in her fingers, and quicker than I can see she's got a spark smoldering in a small pile of leaves and tinder.

"You're quite good at that," I remark, impressed.

"I am dexterous," Dex replies, giving me a little wink.

"Show off." Jackanet snorts.

"He's just jealous because he can't start a fire," Tudie whispers to me, loudly enough for the squire to hear. She's already got her knitting out, and the needles are clacking away in her hands.

Grumbling, Jackanet goes to collect wood while Torvold joins us at the fire's edge with a black pot and a haunch of monster meat.

"I'd like to say that I know the perfect way to prepare chimera-griff, but sadly, I do not," he says with a sheepish grin.

I take a look at the haunch Torvold's holding. It still has a few feathers clinging to it.

"Looks more like poultry than snake. Probably from the eagle portion. I'd go with rosemary," I say, already digging in my pack for the herb. "And lots of salt."

Torvold looks taken aback. "Have you eaten snake, my princess?"

Yes, actually, I have. It's amazing what you'll eat when you've been plunked down in the middle of a horrid fairy tale after being hoodwinked by a diabolical used-book saleswoman. Can't tell Torvold that, obviously.

"At court, once," I say airily. "It's considered a delicacy by some."

Dex and Tudie exchange a look but say nothing to contradict me.

"Indeed?" Torvold replies, considering it. He smiles broadly. "It is fortunate we have you here, then, princess."

I inherit the pot and the monster meat. I'd go wash my hands, but I think it's a little late for that.

5
WHAT IS YOUR QUEST?

I managed to wrestle a semi-palatable meal out of Mr. Stinky. Not something you'd go out of your way to ever eat again, but no one's throwing up. Yet.

"Torvold mentioned you were on a quest, dear?" Tudie asks after she has thoroughly chewed, swallowed, and made certain it stayed down.

"Mmm," I mumble around my stringy mouthful.

I hold an apologetic hand to my mouth as I chew and chew. I'm hoping they'll get bored and move on to another topic of conversation. No such luck. I mentally scramble. What do I know about Princess Pleasant?

"You all know that Asphodel the Evil Sorcerer has demanded my hand in marriage," I say tremulously.

My voice is shaking because I'm nervous, and kind of chilly to be honest, but with my expression partly hidden in the dim firelight, my thin, shaky voice could be construed as distraught. I see Torvold clench his hands into fists across the fire.

"Yes. We've heard," Dex says consolingly. She puts a hand over mine and squeezes.

"No one wants that, dearie," Tudie assures me. Then she laughs. "Whoever you marry would be the next king, wouldn't he?"

"Quite so," I reply. They all look at me expectantly. Where the hell am I going with this? Nowhere. I'm going nowhere.

Why didn't I read the whole book before I signed up for this? Why did I sign up for this in the first place? Sure, my life was a mess. My parents split up, I had to leave L.A. and move to Fresno with my mom and go to a new school. I basically have no friends now. My old friends kept in touch for a bit, but when your lives are going in separate directions, there really isn't that much to talk about anymore. I'm surprised to notice that I'm crying.

"There, there, dearie," Tudie says as she wraps me in a squishy hug. "You're going to get through this. I know it seems hard now, but you are going to make it through. I promise you."

"I'm throwing my life away," I blubber into Fortitude's shoulder. Of course, I'm talking about my actual life now, not Princess Pleasant's, but I really need to cry on someone's shoulder about it.

After I'm cried out, Tudie sits me up again and looks me in the eye. "You can't marry him," she says.

I wipe my eyes and stare at her. What can you say when you and the person you're talking to are having two different conversations?

"Unless you were planning on killing him on your wedding night," Jackanet says softly-but-not-that-softly from the other side of the fire.

"You're out of line," Torvold says. He doesn't raise his voice, but there's a dangerous edge to it.

Jackanet stands and removes his cap. "Milord, after witnessing her—er—creative *handling* of what has become our dinner, I am merely noting that our beloved princess is quite brave, as well as attractive." Jackanet executes a complicated bow in my direction that includes several twirly hand movements. Then he coughs. His cough sounds suspiciously like "concealed weapons!" but Torvold doesn't seem to understand.

"You think it's all well and good for a young lady to offer up herself to a loathsome man?" Dex throws a bit of chimera-griff at him. "She's a person, not bait!"

Jackanet catches the meat and holds it up. "If she treats Asphodel like she did this chimera-griff," he says, shaking it at her, "her *self* will be fine, and the next day we can all wake up singing and dancing!"

"Enough!" Torvold yells. Everyone falls silent. "If we sacrifice the best of ourselves so that the rest may live, what's the point of living at all?" Torvold turns to me and his big, brown eyes melt into mine. "I was chosen to protect Virtue. And I will protect yours, my princess."

He strides away from the fire and into the darkness alone.

After a beat, Jackanet sighs. "He's a good man, my master. Got no common sense, though."

"Lucky for us," Dex retorts, giving a watered-down laugh. Jackanet smiles warmly back at her and nods. They turn to me.

"I suppose you're one of us now," Jackanet tells me.

I don't know what that means, but it's nice to be included. "It's been a long time since I've felt like I've had anyone on my side," I say.

"Whatever happens, whatever you and Father have planned, we'll sort it out together," Tudie says, patting my hand. "Cheer up, dearie. We're not going to let you go through this alone, but you will get through it."

I smile at all of them, because they really have made me feel better even if they have no idea what's really going on.

"Thank you for trying to help," I reply gently. "But I'm the only one who can do this."

I wake the next morning to the sound of bickering.

"It said go *up* the River of Tears to the other side of the Forest of Woe. That means upstream," Dex complains loudly.

I open my eyes. Jackanet and the two White Witches stand in a huddle not too far away from my head, bent over a piece of parchment.

"Up means north," Jackanet disagrees, snatching the parchment from Fortitude's hands and waving it in Dexterity's face.

Dexterity snatches it away from him. "You twit. Up means upriver. How many quests have you gone on?"

"I've been on many quests!" Jackanet insists. He tries to snatch the parchment out of Dexterity's hands, but she's too dexterous, obviously. She holds it away from him and he jumps after it a few times before realizing that his behavior is undignified and gives up.

I sit up.

"Good morning, Princess," says a deep voice.

I turn and see Sir Torvold crouching down by the fire. He hasn't put his chainmail on yet. He's just wearing the leathers and linens that go under it. The neck of his shirt where the strings lace it up has fallen open and I can see copious amounts of collarbone. You wouldn't think collarbones were super sexy, unless you saw them framed by a linen shirt that was casually unlaced at the neck early in the morning and falling open like it could even go down the chest a bit, then maybe even over to show just a hint of the shoulder, and then *whoa*. That is some sexy collarbone.

You know what? I've just figured out why it's so sexy. He's fully dressed, but I know I'm seeing what, in this era, are technically his underthings. He's cooking in medieval lingerie, basically. I blush and look away.

"That depends," I say. "What's for breakfast?"

I couldn't stomach a second round of Mr. Stinky.

Later, when I'm starving, sure. Being squeamish is just silly when you're out in the wild, but I'd have to be stupid hungry to attempt it.

Sir Torvold tilts the pot toward me. "Porridge," he says, smiling as if he guessed I was dreading last night's leftovers. He sniffs the steam and scrunches his nose. "But it's missing something."

I reach into my pillow/satchel and pull out a generous-sized wallet. "Salt," I say, smiling and shaking it.

"That's all salt?" he asks. I grin in answer and kneel down next to him by the fire.

"It's a luxury, I know, but it makes everything better," I say, sprinkling a pinch into the porridge.

He looks back into the pot and stirs. "That's generous of you," he says.

I don't know what to say. Salt is a form of currency here, like gold, only more useful. If he knew I came from a place where we put it on the ground to melt snow in the winter he'd probably freak out. And in fourteen days, I fully intend to be back in that world, throwing salt around like confetti on New Year's, so there's no point in being stingy with what I've got with me. I'm not generous. I'm just leaving. I can't explain that so instead, I sit here awkwardly and listen to Torvold's peanut gallery argue with each other about which way to go while he spoons sticky porridge into five bowls.

"Do you know where you're going?" I ask him quietly.

He nods, grinning. "They love to argue, though. I figured I'll let them have at it for a while."

After a few more moments, Torvold raises his voice pleasantly to cut through the squabbling. "We're going upriver," he announces. "That is where the White Witch Temperance was last seen."

Dex gives Jackanet a smug look. "Shut it," Jackanet grumbles at her, then goes to brush Thunder.

Torvold hands me my bowl. "Your destination lies upriver, then?" he asks, avoiding my eyes. "Then you'll go west?"

I rapidly spoon hot porridge into my mouth rather than answer, but Torvold is waiting for my answer with a strident look on his face.

"We'll all go together for as long as we can," Tudie says briskly. She takes her bowl and sits down next to me.

Dex sits down on my other side. "And who knows? As we travel along things could change. The princess might find that her quest has changed as well."

Torvold seems to brighten with that thought. "Indeed," he says optimistically. He smiles at me, though he's still talking to Dex. "Even now Asphodel the Evil Sorcerer could be gasping his last."

I smile back at him, my cheeks warming, while my breakfast congeals in my bowl. Tudie elbows me. I look away from Torvold and get busy with eating.

After taking care of our personal hygiene issues (which each of us urgently needs after a few spoonsful of medieval porridge) we head out together upriver. This time I insist that the White Witches ride Thunder. Jackanet leads the horse, as Thunder is bred for battle and impossible to control from the saddle unless you are made of solid muscle and wearing spurs. Torvold and I walk beside them.

"How is it you were chosen for this quest, good sir knight?" I ask.

"I'm the only one who can protect them, really," he says, frowning down at his feet.

"Why is that?" I ask, raising an eyebrow. "Surely there are many knights who are great fighters."

"It's his sword, Calx," Dexterity says. "It's the only thing that can kill Asphodel."

"It's not the sword," Jackanet groans, as if they've had this argument a thousand times. "It's the birthmark."

"He's not going to kill the sorcerer with a bloody birthmark!" Fortitude hollers, like she's on her last nerve. Then she puts a shocked hand to her lips. "Excuse me, milady." Nobody waits to see if I'm offended.

"No, Tudie," Dex corrects, "Jackanet means it's *because* of the birthmark Torvold can kill Asphodel with the sword. Sir Torvold has a birthmark shaped like a Puce Pinkerknuckle, which means he's the chosen one who can wield the sword."

"There's no such thing as a Puce Pinkerknuckle." Tudie grumbles.

"It's not the sword! I'm telling you, the birthmark's

poison," Jackanet insists. "Asphodel will touch it and die because it's *not of this world.*"

"He won't touch—" Tudie breaks off for a moment, like what Jackanet just said was so overwhelmingly stupid she doesn't know where to begin. "The sword is not of this world, you idiot. The birthmark just means that Torvold can wield it and the sword is the only thing that can kill Asphodel!"

"Made of sky metal, that sword," Dex adds, winking at me.

"No, it isn't," Tudie says, pinching her lips together. "It was forged in the belly of a dragon."

"Nonsense. How would you get a blacksmith in there?"

"I dunno. It's not of this world."

Jackanet is shaking his head. "No, it's the birthmark that's not from this world. Have either of you even *read* the prophecy?"

"How can the Puce Pinkerknuckle be not of this world? It's on Torvold's backside!" Fortitude shouts.

Torvold shoots me a horrified look, and I have to cover my mouth to keep from doing one of my hideous snort-laughs.

"Puce Pinkerknuckle," Jackanet insists.

"That's not—!" Tudie stops herself again and takes a deep breath.

Torvold holds my elbow and slows his steps. I slow down with him.

"They'll go on like this for another hour at least," he whispers in my ear. We drop back even farther, but they don't notice.

"Is it true?" I ask.

"What? The sword or the birthmark?" he replies, giving me a roguish smile through his blush. And if you've never seen that combination of embarrassed and cheeky before in a guy, I just want to let you know that it is absolutely devastating.

I shake my head and look down to hide the fact that it suddenly feels extremely hot in this corset.

"Is it true that you're the only one who can kill Asphodel?" I ask.

"I have a mark. Don't know what a Pinkerknuckle is, so I suppose it could be one."

"And what about the sword?"

"Calx," he says, like he's saying the name of a friend. He draws his sword and lays it across his arm to show me the blade.

It does not shine. In fact, it is made of a dark, dirty-looking metal, as if it's just been pulled from a fire, except for the edge. All the way around the cutting edge of the blade sparkles. It looks like diamond. I reach out to feel it, and Torvold pulls Calx away quickly.

"It will burn you if you touch it," he warns me.

I frown up at him. "Is it hot?"

"Not to me, but to everyone else, it feels like it was just pulled from the fire." He sheathes his sword. "It's the only weapon Asphodel fears. That is why I was chosen for this quest. I'm the only one who can protect the Virtues from him."

"Huh," I say, remembering something I read once in one of my chemistry books back home. "Calx is the residue left by a burnt mineral."

Torvold smiles. "Yes," he replies, looking at me strangely. "I learned that from an alchemist. How did you know?"

Yeah. How would I know that? Not a lot of chemistry classes in Lucitopia.

"There's not much to do in a tower besides read," I say.

"You can read?" he asks, surprised.

I nod and shrug at the same time, like it's no big deal, but it is a big deal. There are probably five people in this whole world who can read, and as a person of the female persuasion, I'm not supposed to be one of them. Unbelievably sexist, but also true.

"I can as well," he says, like he's admitting something he's supposed to keep hidden for manly reasons. "I was not supposed to be a knight." He looks down and stops himself from continuing.

I tilt my head to the side, so I can see his expression better. "What were you supposed to be?" I ask.

He lifts his head to answer and takes a breath and... wow. We are extremely close together. Like, I'm almost wearing his clothes right now. There's a slight breeze that blows a tress of my shampoo commercial-perfect hair gently across my cheek. Torvold catches it and smooths it back from my face. He leaves his hand there for a moment, barely touching the edge of my jaw.

"A-hem!"

Torvold and I jump apart. The peanut gallery has come back for us. Jackanet is glaring at me, Dex is trying not to giggle, and Tudie looks a little worried, but not surprised.

"I think we should all stay together, don't you, dearie?" Tudie says as she comes back, takes my hand, and walks beside me for the rest of the morning.

That was close. Torvold's the hero of this book. Everybody's rooting for Torvold. Readers aren't going to like me if they think I'm toying with his emotions while I wait for a real boy to kiss me. I have to be more careful.

From now on, no more fraught pauses where I stand there staring at him like he's a pint of ice cream and I'm a warm spoon. Torvold and I are just going to be friends. Cohorts. Co-questers. And that's *it*.

6
STUFFED UP HER CHIMNEY

We reach the edge of the Forest of Woe by sunset, which is a terrible time to get anywhere in Lucitopia. It's not dark enough to arrive unseen, but it won't be light out long enough to put some real distance between you and whoever decides to start chasing you.

Late afternoon is good. I can work with a late afternoon arrival, but evening? Just terrible.

In Lucitopia, there aren't gradual changes from one kind of scenery to another. When a forest ends, it ends. Just like on a map. We stay hidden in the line of trees.

"That must be Temperance's cottage," Dex whispers.

Laid out in front of us are the Fields of Plenty. Right on the edge of Woe and Plenty is a small, sturdy-looking cottage. The wattle and daub walls are whitewashed, the shutters are a sensible black, and the thatched roof is full, but not overstuffed like in some fairy tales. A squat windmill churns the River of Tears, turning all that sorrow into labor, and around it pools a medium-sized pond with some very ordinary ducks floating on top.

"All of you wait here," Torvold tells us. "I'll go scout for bandits."

He crouches down low and disappears into the waving field of some kind of grain. I'm not a farmer, but the crop definitely waves, so I'm going to guess rye? Barley?

We see Torvold appear again next to one of the windows. He looks inside. He sneaks around to the front door. He lifts the latch and opens it.

And goes flying through the air.

He's thrown twenty feet away from the cottage and lands flat on his back. He doesn't get up. I know it has to be a spell, which are illusion, but I'm sprinting alongside Jackanet anyway. We both get to him at the same time. Jackanet throws himself down on his knees next to Torvold.

"Master! Are you injured?" he asks pleadingly.

Torvold doesn't move.

"Torvold," I say. Not a twitch. I crouch down next to him and put my hand on his chest. I can feel his heart beating and I don't see any blood. But if he got hit with a spell, why isn't he screaming? "Torvold, wake up," I say more sharply.

I see motion by the cottage door out of the corner of my eye, and without thinking, I turn and throw one of the blades from my bodice. I hit my mark perfectly, pinning her to the doorframe by her clothes.

Wait a second.

She's absolutely gorgeous. She has dark skin, long curly black hair, killer bod, maybe in her early twenties, and *not* a bandit. The woman looks from her pinned sleeve and back to me in surprise. It's a white sleeve. I think I just threw a knife at Temperance. I grimace and get up.

"Excellent throw, Princess!" she says.

"I'm really sorry," I say, approaching her to pull out the blade. Tudie and Dex join us at a jog, and Thunder trails behind them.

"You didn't even nick me," Temperance says, eyes still wide with surprise.

"I think that was more luck than anything else," I say, tugging the blade out of the doorframe. "Sorry about your dress."

"Not at all," she replies cheerily. "I have more inside just like it."

"Are you both done discussing your wardrobes?" Jackanet interrupts. He gestures frantically to Torvold's unconscious body.

I turn back to Temperance with a worried look on my face.

"Oh, he'll be fine," she says with a wave of her hand. "He got hit pretty hard, but he'll sleep it off."

"Does it hurt?" I ask.

"No," she replies, grinning. "It feels wonderful."

She narrows her eyes at me and then nods as if she just figured something out.

She turns back to Torvold and mutters, "Who's a big boy? We're probably going to need that horse to help drag him inside unless we take the chainmail off first. Right! Who wants to undress him?"

Jackanet unbuckles Torvold's mail and slides it off of him. Jackanet has to put his shoulder under it to lift it and carry it into the cottage. Must weigh forty or fifty pounds.

"That helped, but there is still a lot of fine young man here to carry," Temperance says, in a very intemperate way, I might add. "Everyone, choose a body part."

I end up with a foot. Between the five of us, we manage to wrangle Torvold into the small, neat cottage and dump him on top of Temperance's bed.

"We should probably take his boots off," I say after I notice the lovely floral coverlet. I reach for the boot nearest me, but Jackanet shoos me away.

"Off, off," he mutters. I guess he's still upset about seeing Torvold fly through the air like that. It *was* really scary. I'm still shaking a little, to be honest.

Temperance touches Jackanet on the shoulder. "He'll be fine. He's having wonderful dreams right now, I assure you," she says.

There's something about the way she talks that takes the worry and the irritation away. Even Jackanet, who does not warm to newcomers quickly, can't help but give in and join us by the fire for some tea. She's got cookies. I haven't had sugar since I got here, which might explain my crystal-clear complexion, but right now I'm not worried about a breakout.

After we've all dug into her butter cookies with jam and gone back for seconds, Temperance settles back, stirring her chamomile tea and looking us over.

"Now may I ask why the young knight was peeking in my window?" she says good-naturedly.

"Oh, we've come to save you, dearie," Tudie says, patting her knee.

Tudie goes on to explain who they are, and about Torvold's quest. She leaves me mostly out of it, saying only that they encountered me in great need and now we travel together. While Fortitude soldiers on through the back-story, Temperance eyes me over the rim of her teacup, sizing me up. There's no judgment in her, not in a mean way, but she is measuring me. Like a doctor checking my height, she just wants to know how much I've grown.

"So, you see, Temperance, it's vitally important you come with Torvold, as he is the only one who can protect you," Tudie finishes soundly.

"You think I'm Temperance?" the White Witch asks. She laughs warmly and shakes her head. "No, I'm not Temperance, although she was here a few weeks ago. She loves to stop in to lecture me every now and again, but she never stays long."

"Who are you, then?" Jackanet blurts out.

The White Witch smiles at him. "You know me," she

says in that dulcet voice of hers. Jackanet's face goes soft and he leans back, nodding a little.

"Yes, milady," he whispers.

She stands, and I get a whiff of her perfume. Apples and vanilla, magnolia and spice, and something animal underneath that's kind of gnarly, but I keep trying to get another whiff of it anyway.

"I'll tend the horse," she says. "You should all get some rest."

I suddenly feel like I can't keep my eyes open. I want to ask who she is, but I'm too busy finding a nice spot on the floor to curl up on. I'll ask tomorrow.

I wake to a muffled thump.

A slippery, acid feeling floods my stomach. I listen and hear other ears listening for mine. I know you're wondering how ears can hear other ears listening, but just trust me. When there are no electrical appliances charging, no planes flying overhead, no neighbors of any kind for miles, and you are a hotter commodity than a mature IRA, you get really good at hearing the different kinds of dark. This dark has ears in it, and they are listening to see if mine are listening back.

Which they are. Which those ears probably know at this point.

It's a race now. A stealthy, tiptoeing, sliding your-daggers out slowly kind of race. I peel myself off the floor and pad over Dex's sleeping body, then skootch around Tudie. I have to dart from there to get to the darkest shadow in the corner by the window without passing through the moonlight coming through it. When I get there, I turn and lean my back up against the wall.

I feel something tall and firm behind me, but it's definitely not a wall. A big arm crosses my body and a warm hand cups my mouth. Lips press against my ear.

"Shh," Torvold whispers. Instant shivers go down my spine, which is pressed right up against his chest.

I nod, and he lets go of my mouth, but that hand floats down to my shoulder and holds there, keeping my back flat against him so we both fit inside this shadow. His back is pressed to the wall and he cranes his head to the side to look out the window. I look out with him, sure he can feel my heart beating in my throat.

He tilts his head down until his lips touch my ear again. "There are four outside and one on the roof," he whispers so softly that if he weren't this close, I couldn't hear him.

I nod again and focus on the fireplace. The fire went out hours ago, but I can hear a faint scratching in there.

Tilting my head back so my lips can reach his ear I whisper, "He's coming down the chimney."

I slide one of my sleeve daggers out, point to my chest to indicate myself, and then I point to the fireplace.

Torvold leans slightly to the side so he can look me in the eye. He's surprised for a moment, then he smiles. It's a sly smile. I think I impressed him. It feels pretty good to have a monster-slaying hero like Torvold think I might be kind of a hero, too.

I'm supposed to be moving right now. I just indicated that the chimney was my post, and that's where I should be headed, but instead, I'm still leaning back against Torvold and I'm tilted to the side so I can stare up at him. He is mighty comfortable. And beautiful.

And that's enough of that.

I slink out of our hiding place and dance over the sleeping bodies. I get to the fireplace and stand beside it. Torvold has already made it to the cottage door, and he's looking across the room at me. I signal that I'm ready, and he yanks the door open and runs out with a mighty battle cry.

Total hero.

Everyone in the cottage wakes, and they all jump up. I wave frantically at everyone, finger to my lips, and then point at the fireplace so they know that someone is coming down it.

"There must be bandits outside!" I yell. "To the *windows*!" I make a shooing motion with my hand to get them to go.

Jackanet understands what I'm doing. He starts corralling Tudie and Dex toward the other side of the cottage. "Ho! Torvold the Bold fights for our lives! Let us watch!" he yells like the stiffest high school kid with one line in the show.

I grimace. Jackanet grimaces back. We'll never win any Oscars.

Old Saint Dick stuck up the chimney knows this is his cue to climb down, sneak up behind someone watching the show outside, take a hostage, and then the bandits would have us.

But this ain't my first rodeo. I ready my dagger in one hand. I grab a copper pan off the mantel and hold it in the other, just to be sure.

I see a foot set down in the grate.

There's something wrong with it. Actually, make that a couple of somethings. First of all, it doesn't have a boot on it. Second, it's got really long toenails. Third, it's a putrid green-grey color.

A matching putrid hand snakes down and clasps the edge of the fireplace, and then a gaunt face appears. It has two bulbous, lidless eyes and no nose. Or rather, it had a nose once, but that must have rotted off because instead this guy just has those long holes like you see on a skull. Most of his lips are gone, too. But that's not strange. That's just another extra on *The Walking Dead*.

He pokes his head and shoulders out, now that he sees everyone looking out the windows with their backs to the fireplace like a bunch of rubes, and I can see the side of his neck has slits on it. Like gills. They open and suck in air. I think he tasted me, because his head snaps around and he looks right at me. I immediately clunk him with the copper pan.

He makes this congested orca call, think *Flipper* but way more phlegm, and he lunges for me. I whack him again. He crawls a little closer to me. I give him another clang upside the head. He twitches, and yep, that does it for me. I whale on him a good six or seven times. Then I take a beat to readjust my grip. I choke the handle in both hands and I go to town on him like I'm chopping wood.

He doesn't move. The rest of his body slithers down to fall on top of him as if his bones are made of rubber. Really stinky rubber. Should have dubbed him Jingle Smells. I whack him just *one more time* for good measure.

By now the rest of the gang are standing next to me with shocked looks on their faces—except for Jackanet. He knows I've got rage. We get a snoot full of hot garbage stench and pinch our noses closed. We all sound like ducks when we talk.

"This is terrible," Jackanet quacks, gesticulating wildly.

"I know. He'll stink up Temperance's cottage for weeks," I quack, looking for the White Witch who is definitely *not* Temperance. Where is she?

"No, no, you don't understand!" Jackanet stomps a foot. I giggle. He looks and sounds like a big baby. "That's a *drawl!*" he quacks.

"A *drawl*?" I quack back. "What's that?"

"Not a *drawl*," Jackanet lets go of his nose momentarily, "a Thrall!" He pinches his nose closed again.

"Oh, well, I think I got some Thrall on my skirt," I

quack, pointing at a little spatter at the hem. I notice that the Thrall is not moving. "Do you think I killed him?" I ask Tudie anxiously. I've never killed anything even remotely human-shaped before.

"I hope so," she quacks. "Put the poor thing out of his misery."

"Don't take your eyes off that one," Jackanet quacks as he hustles to the door. "I've got to help Torvold!"

Jackanet throws himself out the cottage door, and Dex sighs mightily and follows him. "I'd better make sure he doesn't get killed," she quacks.

I know this is all very serious stuff, but it's hard to feel grim when everyone is quacking.

I listen for the sounds of fighting outside, but all I can hear is Jackanet calling for his master. I look at Tudie.

"Should I be worried?" I quack at her.

Tudie shrugs. "Probably," she quacks back.

"Where is our hostess?" I ask, looking around, thinking she might be in danger.

"Hopefully far away from here," Tudie replies fervently.

"Should we be worried she's been taken?"

Tudie shakes her head with a knowing smile. "You can't take her, dearie. She can only be given."

Weird. I'm about to ask more, but I hear Torvold calling out in the distance and I strain my ears to listen to him. A few moments after that, I hear him run back into the yard. He's scolding Jackanet.

"You mustn't let her out here! Get back inside, Dex, please," he says.

A moment later, Jackanet and Dex are pushed inside by Torvold. There are black splatters on his white linen shirt and his chest is heaving. That's a lot of chest to heave, by the way. He comes directly to me.

"Are you injured?" he asks. His eyes are big and soft, though his voice is rough. "Did you touch it at all, or did you get it with just the blade of the dagger?"

"No," I quack. I realize I'm still holding my nose. I am utterly ridiculous. I drop my hand. "I didn't use my dagger, I used this." I hold up the copper pan.

Torvold lets out a sigh and clasps my upper arm. For just a moment he drops his forehead to touch mine. Then he jerks away and goes to the rubbery heap of moldering scabs and fishy phlegm on the hearth. He raises Calx.

"I think it's dead," I interject, but he cuts its head off without pausing.

The Thrall bursts into flames. There's a quick, agonized scream as it twitches and shrivels and turns to powdery white-grey ash faster than if it were made of tissue paper.

Torvold sighs with relief. "*Now* it's dead," he says, looking back up at me. "I'm so sorry. I never would have left you to face this alone if I knew it was a Thrall. I ran out, thinking they were men." He combs a hand through his hair. "I should have watched them longer, but I...you woke and I..." he trails off. Looking at me.

Everyone is silent. I shrug. "All is well, Sir Torvold," I say quietly. "I managed it."

I look down at my pan and notice that the goo from the Thrall that was on it has burnt away as well. And so has the spatter on the hem of my dress. I look at Torvold's shirt and notice that the black marks on it are actually burn holes. Even the stench is gone. It burned away.

I've lived in Lucitopia for nearly a year and I've never heard mention of a Thrall.

"Someone please explain what a Thrall is," I say. "And tell me why I've never heard of one before."

They share a look like no one wants to have this conversation.

Dex is the first to speak up. "They are the Thrall of Asphodel," she says. "They were people once, but to avoid death, they gave themselves to Asphodel. In exchange, he changes them. He controls them completely and they cannot die by any agent of this land. Even their touch is poison."

I nod in understanding, but I'm still wary.

"That explains why my pan was ineffectual, but they shriveled when touched by Calx. That also explains why Sir Torvold was so afraid when he realized he'd left me to deal with one on my own, unwarned as I am about their poisonous touch." I try to meet every single one of their gazes, but they all look away from mine. "Yet methinks there is some other foul mischief you have not revealed."

"You've been in your tower for a long time, dearie,"

Tudie says, shifting from foot to foot. "And then all of a sudden you set out on this quest." She stops and looks at Dex.

Dex starts over. "You haven't seen your father in a while," she says reasonably. "And there have been a lot of changes."

They pause. "And?" I urge.

"You know he had to leave the palace, don't you?" Tudie says hesitantly.

"And there was that hag who drained him dry," Dex adds.

"What happened to my father?" I demand. I know they're talking about the king, and not my real dad, but they might as well be.

Before I came to Lucitopia a year ago I hadn't seen my father in eight months. He used to be a big player in Hollywood, but he lost his job when the studio "restructured" (a.k.a. lost a boatload of money when a film turned into a billion-dollar flop) and they fired half of the mid-level executives. My dad lost his house. The woman he left my mother for, a little starlet who was gorgeous on the outside and a hag on the inside, took pretty much everything else he owned.

My dad's not perfect. Scratch that. My dad is a horse's behind, but he's still my dad and I am worried about him. The doctors don't measure his blood pressure in systolic over diastolic anymore, but in how many days away from a heart attack he is.

"If you have word of my father, you must tell me," I say. I have to stop to swallow the lump in my throat. "I haven't seen him in so long." Why is it hard to say that? I must really miss him. I thought I never wanted to see him again, but I guess I do.

"There's been talk that the king has become a Thrall of Asphodel," Jackanet admits sadly.

"Anything he might have told you," Dex begins.

"Any quest he might have given you, is most likely the will of Asphodel," Tudie finishes.

Torvold takes a step toward me, but he stops himself and says, "Don't marry him." His voice is husky and low. "Please, princess."

Jackanet turns to Torvold. "Milord, if she could get *close* to Asphodel by accepting his proposal of marriage, she could be the only one—"

"It's a trap!" Torvold thunders.

"It most certainly is, but hear me out," Jackanet pleads. Torvold pivots on his heel and walks out of the cottage toward the stables.

"Did you *see* her with the *pan*?" Jackanet yells after him, but it's no use. Torvold will not listen.

I have to sit. I meander over to a chair and sink down into it. "I don't know what to do," I say quietly.

No one answers me.

7
WHO, ME? JEALOUS?

I wake to the low, grey light of predawn.

I have thirteen days left. Hopefully less, if I can swing it. I'm sick of pretending to be Princess Pleasant. I'm starting to feel—not like a liar, exactly, because I haven't actually lied.

Okay, yes, I feel like a liar!

But the very nature of my predicament is based on me pretending to be someone I'm not. It's not my fault it's starting to feel real. And it's not my fault that Torvold is so upset I'm supposedly on a dangerous quest that I never specifically spelled out to anyone. He just assumed.

Anyway, whatever quest I could be on would be a dangerous one, given the state of things here in Lucitopia. Just because he's tearing himself up inside, thinking I'm going to sacrifice myself to an evil, undead sorcerer isn't much worse than me…I don't know…fighting a dragon or something.

Right?

I stare up at the ceiling. I'm on the edge of the bed with the pretty floral-patterned bedspread. Dex is next to me, Tudie is next to her, and Jackanet is at our feet. I roll over onto my stomach and face Torvold lying on the floor next to me. He's wide awake. Calx is in his hand as if he spent the night with it unsheathed.

"Did you sleep at all?" I whisper to him.

He shrugs in a non-committal way. "You?" he whispers back.

I shrug back.

"Are you frightened the Thrall will return?" he asks.

I frown, thinking about my sleepless night. "I'm doubting my course of action," I admit honestly.

He smiles up at me. His tired eyes look relieved. "Good."

I take a moment to really look him over. And not in a hormonal way, for a change. This is a guy who just spent the night on the floor, holding a sword that probably weighs about twenty pounds, after crossing a forest and fighting battles, all so he can protect other people. If I want to be the hero of my own story, I'd better start taking my cues from him.

"If you had a chance to strike at someone who had destroyed so much and hurt so many, wouldn't you take the risk?" I ask him.

He swallows hard and looks away. "It matters not what I would do. You are too important to endanger yourself, princess."

"I'm no more important than anyone in this room," I whisper. "And less than some." He looks back at me, eyes burning, ready to argue, but I don't let him. "I'm handy with small blades, but I'll need to be prepared for any misfortune in order to confront Asphodel." My mouth goes dry, because now I'm actually considering this madness. "You could teach me."

He shakes his head, and it hurts me that he won't teach me. I look away from him, and I'm about to turn over but he reaches up to stop me.

"I know you're brave and I know you can fight," he whispers, and again I see that impressed look on his face. "But I'm the only one who can kill Asphodel." He touches Calx beside him to remind me.

"Oh, that's right," I mutter, face falling. "I'm not the bearer of the Puce Pinkerknuckle." I look at him mischievously. "Tudie doesn't believe it exists."

He grins at me and moves as if to roll over and show me his butt. "Do you want to see it?"

"No." I giggle quietly, smacking his chest. He captures my hand and keeps it.

"I don't know if it's really there or not," he jokes, tugging me toward him. "I'm not an owl, you know? I can't see my own..."

I'm trying not to laugh too hard or fall out of the bed.

I don't want to wake the others just yet. I want him to myself for as long as I can have him.

Because I know Torvold won't get close enough to kill Asphodel until about three-quarters of the way through the book. It's the one thing I know for certain. Torvold the Bold heroically challenges Asphodel at the battle of Knob Knoll, and he dies.

Torvold sees my mirth dissolve and he holds my hand tightly against his chest.

"Aid me in my quest and abandon your own." He stops himself like he knows what he's asking is tantamount to treason, but he sticks to his guns and continues. "You could save many lives, but the one thing you cannot do is kill Asphodel. Please, Princess."

"But Jackanet thinks I could..."

"Jackanet is searching for any way to spare me," Torvold interrupts gently. "He is the one who suggested to the other knights that I protect the Virtues, rather than ride out and demand single combat against Asphodel."

I frown. "Why would he do that?"

"He's worried I'll lose," Torvold says. He rubs my fingers in his. "I was sent on this quest as a diversion, but I know there is only one end to this war."

And so do I. Knob Knoll is the end, and it is also Torvold's. I've had plenty of reason to dislike the author of this book in the past—the ax in the face spell comes to mind—but never so much as now.

We stay like that for a long time. Me looking down on him from the edge of the bed, and him holding my hand against his chest until the room turns pink with newborn light.

The others wake. We rattle around the cottage, looking for food, heating water to freshen up, and generally pulling ourselves together before we head out again.

Torvold goes to the stables to feed Thunder while the rest of us rob the joint.

"Who was our hostess, and where did she go?" I ask as I ransack her kitchen. I look up and notice Tudie, Dex, and Jackanet sharing a look. "What?" I ask, throwing my hands up.

"You didn't recognize her?" Dex asks.

"Should I have?" I reply.

"Come on now," Jackanet says, disbelievingly. His eyebrows have practically disappeared into his hairline.

"What?" I repeat, this time feeling put-upon. "I didn't recognize her! Who is she?"

"Just like a woman," Jackanet grumbles as he turns away from me. He starts gathering up provisions with a little more force than necessary. "She knocked Torvold halfway to his maker, but you? Didn't even recognize her."

I look around. Everyone is suspiciously busy at the moment. "I have no idea what's going on," I announce.

"It's all right, dearie," Tudie says gently. "You'll know who she is when you *know*. No one can explain it to you. We'll have to leave it at that."

"It's comforting to know she's still out there," Jackanet says quietly, almost reverently. "I wonder if the other two are faring as well."

"What other two?" I ask, growing testy. "She's part of a set, I'm assuming?"

"The Big Three," Dex says, nodding. "Without them, Lucitopia is lost."

We are back on the road before midday, and though we are following an actual road across the Fields of Plenty, I don't know where it leads. Or where I'm going. Or what I'm doing with my life in general.

Torvold has fallen back with Jackanet, and the two of them are deep in discussion. I hover for a while but give up when I see that they are not about to break apart.

"Do you know where we're going?" I ask Dex.

"Our hostess last night—" she begins.

"You're really not going to tell me who she was?" I ask, interrupting.

"I can't," Dex says, sounding legitimately sorry. "It's one of those life revelation things. You've got to go through it yourself. Now, do you want me to answer your question or not?"

"Yes," I sigh, rolling my eyes.

"Our hostess told Torvold that another of the Big Three is traveling with some minstrels. While our hostess never really dies, which I've unfortunately come to learn, the other two in the Big Three can."

I frown as I walk. "When did Torvold talk to her?" I ask.

Dex shrugs. "After we fell asleep, I expect. He must have awoken and the two of them shared words."

I can't help but think about how pretty she was, and how amazing she smelled, and—not going to lie—how incredible her body was. She was also quite clear that she found him attractive.

"Huh," I say, glancing back at Torvold.

Dex squints at me. "Huh, what?" she asks.

I walk casually. Bored, even. "It's just, he and I spoke before the rest of you woke and he didn't mention that he'd *shared words* with her." Okay, that sounded jealous even to me.

Dex suppresses a smile. "Must have slipped his mind."

I'm stewing. It's silly to keep thinking about this. There are other ways for me to spend my time, like figuring out what my quest is going to be. I can't follow Torvold around, trusting him to come up with a quest while I tag along. If I'm going to get out of here, and I am getting out of here, I have to stop going with the flow and be an active character. I can't let some guy make all the decisions for me. I hate female characters like that, the ones who conveniently appear when the main character needs to unburden himself of some exposition or when he needs to go rescue something in the third act. They are all over the place in fantasy novels. It's like, get your own quest, sweetie, and stop waiting around for Mr. Muscles to validate you.

Tudie comes alongside me. She's practically jogging to keep up. I realize I must have pulled away from the group.

"We've all stopped for lunch," she says, gesturing back the way we came.

I stop and glance back. I can't even see anyone. "How far back?" I ask. The Fields of Plenty have turned into rolling hills, scattered with clumps of trees. At some point, while I stomped along, the scenery changed.

"Er—far," she says, grimacing.

"I have food in my pack," I say, feeling sheepish. "Doesn't make sense for us to go all the way back now."

"No, it doesn't," she agrees. Tudie takes me by the arm and walks a little with me further up the road. "Let's find a nice place to sit in the shade and talk over whatever's bothering you."

We walk along in silence for a while, heading for a copse of trees just a bit off the road, when I get a funny feeling. It's the *duck* feeling. Not quite as serious as the *run like hell* feeling, but in the same ballpark. I've learned to listen to feelings like that, so I duck and pull Tudie down with me.

I shush her before she can yelp or ask a stupid question like *what's going on* when I obviously don't know what's going on because I'm crouching down behind a bush.

We both hear voices coming from the copse of trees. Then we hear a rough voice being raised, followed by splintering and a discordant twanging sound. Something musical just got broken.

"It could be the minstrels we're looking for," Tudie guesses hopefully. She's keeping her voice down, though.

"Possibly," I allow. "But I don't think they'd smash their instruments."

"Bandits, then," Tudie decides. "Do you think they saw us coming up the road?"

I shrug. "If they did, they'll send someone to get us."

"Should we run back for Torvold?"

"They'll *definitely* see us then, and if they have horses, they'll catch us. Our best bet is to stay hidden, get closer, and try to find out if it's safe to approach them or not."

Tudie nods once, ready to go into stealth mode, and she and I creep through the bushes toward the voices until we're close enough to see what's going on.

We find two festively painted carts among the trees. Both have been ransacked, and one is missing a wheel. Sparkly costumes, wigs, and make-up pots are tossed across the leaflitter. Tudie and I frown at each other and keep our heads down as we get closer.

We peek into a small clearing among the trees and see seven rough men standing in a strategic circle. They are definitely bandits, they have horses, and they've got a bunch of underfed, pale, and arty-looking people tied up on the ground.

One of the captives is set apart from the rest. She's only about seven years old. She has long, straight, black hair and almond-shaped eyes. And she's wearing a white dress.

8

IS THAT A HEDGEHOG IN YOUR POCKET?

The biggest, meanest-looking bandit is moving about the inside of the circle, soapboxing to the tied-up minstrels. A shattered lute lays next to an unconscious man who is bleeding from the head.

"Look 'ere," the biggest bandit says, "The rest of you can go. We just want the White Witch. But first, we need you to tell us where you found her. Is that so hard?"

"We'll tell you nothing!" shouts a redheaded kid in a bright green tunic.

One of the other bandits gives him a cuff, but he puts a little too much pepper in his swing. The redhead falls to the ground in a heap, unconscious.

"Sorry," the bandit says sheepishly.

"You can't keep knocking everyone out," the big leader says. "Who am I going to question then!?"

"Didn't mean to." He slinks away from the red and green heap.

The biggest bandit turns back to the remaining minstrels. "Maybe you'd like us to bring you to Asphodel?" he says. "Because if you don't tell us where you saw this little witch's friends, we'll *have* to bring you to him. And nobody wants that, right?"

He spins around, throwing his arms out wide and smiling.

Ew. Asphodel obviously does not include dental in his henchmen plan.

"You tell us where the other White Witches are, we make more money for bringing them to Asphodel, and you get to keep your souls," Raging Gingivitis is saying in his most reasonable voice. "How 'bout it?"

I've seen enough. I pull Tudie back until she and I can speak without being heard.

"We can't leave her. She's one of the Big Three," Tudie says. "She's too important—far more important than me. We must save her."

It's not like I was going to leave her. She's just a kid. However, I was going to suggest we hide until dark and then run back to get Torvold. But now that Fortitude herself is telling me to knuckle up, I do. I swing my pack off my back and put it down between us.

"We need a plan. I've got some spells on me."

I pull out a small tie-string bag and place each spell gently on the ground between us. There's a yellow one the size of a baseball, a silver one the size of a softball, and a tiny brown one the size of a marble.

"What do they do?"

I point to each in order and name what's in them. "Bees, bear trap, and hedgehog."

"What's so terrible about the hedgehog?"

"I think he's rabid," I say. Tudie makes a doubtful face. "It's the best I could get! Where are *your* spells, by the way?" I say, feeling put upon.

"All right, all right." Tudie relents. "Put the rodent away. I think we can manage with the bees and the bear trap."

I tuck the tiny hedgehog spell into my skirt pocket so I don't lose it, and offer Tudie a choice between the other two. She takes the bees.

"Okay, so what we have to do is..." I trail off when I see Tudie look over my shoulder and stiffen. "There's a bandit right behind me, isn't there?"

"Two," Tudie replies regretfully.

I turn and see two scruffy-looking men. I don't recognize them from the circle in the clearing. They must be the look-outs.

"What you have to do, pretty, is stand up and come join the party," drawls the bandit behind me.

"Join the party," the other one parrots, guffawing.

They've got a smarmy way about them. I've had plenty of time to get acquainted with their type in the post-Knob Knoll version of Lucitopia. These are the kind of guys who start carrying off all the women under twenty after the White Witches are dead.

"Bees," I say to Tudie, standing slowly to give her cover.

"Bees?" she repeats. Then she gets it. "Oh, bees!" She throws the spell and it hits the guffawing bandit right in the face.

"My eyes!" he starts screaming. "I'm not supposed to get bees in them!"

The other bandit tackles me before I can throw the bear trap. I roll with him and pull him against me, clasping my arms tightly around his neck (despite the full-frontal assault of his BO) so I can get at the blade I've got tucked up my sleeve. I pull it out and let go of his head. He rears back and sees that I'm about to stab him in the eye. He moves up and to the side just enough that all I do is skewer the fleshy part of his ear. My blade goes right through it and dangles there, like a giant and very goth piercing.

Having a knife in his ear is enough to get him to fall off me, though, and luckily, he lands right on the bear trap. BO starts kicking and flailing and howling like crazy.

"Run!" I yell, jumping up and grabbing Tudie.

She digs in her heels. "We can't leave."

I throw my head back and growl, "Virtue is a pain!" I turn her around and give her a little push away from danger. "You run and get Torvold, I'll get the girl!"

I double-check my bodice for my blades as I scurry

through the underbrush and head back to the clearing. I need a plan. Plan, plan-a-plan-a-plan-plan.

I don't have a plan, and I'm at the clearing. Instead of seven bandits, there are now four. That's good in that there are fewer bandits for me to fight here in the clearing, but bad because that means there are three bandits that have been sent to find out what the yelling is about. I hope Tudie is a fast runner.

I hear a man's blood-curdling scream that ends in a gurgle from the brush behind me. I'm pretty good at identifying screams after my long tenure in Lucitopia, and I think that was Bees in the Eyes dying a bloody death. Spells can't kill. They're only illusion. Something else is going on.

Raging Gingivitis sends out one more guy to check on the others. I hide behind the tree while he runs past me and then start psyching myself up.

Gingivitis is having a little conference with his two remaining cohorts. He's yelling at them, and they're leaning back. Apparently, Raging Gingivitis' last name is Halitosis. I edge around the clearing, keeping low, until I get near to where the White Witch is tied up on the ground. But there isn't enough cover for me to cut her bonds without the bandits seeing me.

It's time to get heroic. I step out, fully exposed.

"Ho there!" I yell.

I unleash the hedgehog.

It lands right in the middle of the bandits' huddle, and straight away I know this spell is different. I can't see the whole hedgehog, but I can see its furry little outline as it leaps and scurries in a frantic tumble of quills and rabies.

It's a group spell. Fancy.

All three of the bandits experience the same thing at the same time, and apparently, it's bad. They start pushing at the faint outline, screaming, "Get it off! Get it off!" in a perfect chorus of terror.

I take my blade and cut the White Witch's bonds.

"That was marvelous!" she says, jumping up. She gestures to my knife. "May I?" she asks.

I hand it to her and she runs over to the other minstrels and starts cutting their bonds. Now that she's at it, I take out another blade and go help her. I guess it would be very un-classy to leave the rest of them here like that, but that hedgehog isn't going to last forever. I paid practically nothing for it.

Unfortunately, I'm right. By the time we get the medieval drama club free, Gingivitis has pushed through the worst of the spell and he stumbles over to grab onto the White Witch. She screams and jabs at him with my knife, but she's not the stabby type. And she's, like, *seven*, so arm strength is an issue.

I make a move to run at them, but Gingivitis holds my stolen blade up to the little White Witch's throat.

And now I'm pissed. It's bad enough that thugs like this are after Dex and Tudie, but she's just a kid.

"Let her go!" I snarl at him.

"Or you'll what?" he says, taunting me. He's still

getting gnawed on by the hedgehog, but he's got such a huge wellspring of naturally occurring jerk in him that it can't help but bubble to the surface in the form of banter. He leers at me. "You're an interesting one, aren't you?"

"Let go of that little girl and I'll show you how interesting," I promise.

I'm in a crouch and I'm starting to come around. I'm going to try to flank him while my disease-riddled compadre still has some steam in him. I've palmed another blade from my dress and I'm hiding it in the folds of my skirt, but the other two guys are starting to recover now. I'm going to be in a lot of trouble in a second.

I hear footsteps running up fast behind me. I look just in time to see Torvold, turned into a bolt of pure fury, as he slashes through the two bandits behind me.

"That's far enough!" Gingivitis screams frantically. The little witch gives a girlish shriek as the blade cuts a tiny bit into her skin.

Torvold comes to an abrupt halt next to me. "You all right, Princess?" he asks. His voice is low, and his teeth are bared.

"Fine," I say crisply. "Except I really don't like him."

I might be crazy, but I think half of Torvold's mouth just twitched up into a smile.

"You two a couple, then?" Gingivitis says, wagging his eyebrows at Torvold. "She's a game one. I bet she gives you a run for it, though, doesn't she?"

I can feel Torvold's temper getting away from him.

Gingivitis can see it, too.

"I've got a game for you," I say before Gingivitis can push Torvold into making a mistake. "You let go of the girl, and I throw a blade right between your eyes."

"You're just bluffing," Gingivitis says.

"Your men are dead," Torvold says, his temper restored. "You're all alone in this. I've taken your horses, your provisions, and the only weapon you have is a dagger. You will never make it back to Asphodel alive."

What a *gangsta*.

Torvold eases to the left and I edge more toward the right. If we split up, one of us might be able to get behind him. Gingivitis starts backing up, trying to keep the two of us in his sights.

"Stop right there," Gingivitis growls again, and he squeezes the little girl closer to him. She whimpers, and I try a different tactic.

I see a lump just behind Gingivitis. The lump is the unconscious red-headed minstrel in green. He's blended in down there with the leaflitter. I hold both my hands up and let the blade I've palmed slip to the ground. I take one slow step toward the hostage situation.

"Do you know who I am, sirrah?" I ask the bandit. He frowns, his eyes darting between me and Torvold. He takes a step back. I take another step forward and smile brightly. "I'm Princess Pleasant."

"Pull the other one," he tells me, disbelievingly.

"I am," I insist, taking another step. "And if it's gold

you're after, I have coffers full of it."

He takes another step back. "You do look rather like her," he admits.

"Just let me have the child," I say sweetly. I take one last step. "That's all I care about."

He takes that final step back and stumbles over the red-headed boy.

"Torvold!" I yell, but he's already two steps ahead of me.

Torvold catches the White Witch in his arms and turns away from the bandit, shielding the girl with his body.

Gingivitis pops back up on his feet before I can get a dagger out of my garters (stupid petticoats) and he dashes into the trees. I'm a few hundred yards after him when I hear the distinct sound of horse hooves pounding the ground. A few moments more and I catch a glimpse of him through the brush, and then he breaks the tree line and I can see him riding off the road and across the rolling hills.

I stand there, watching him disappear toward the setting sun.

"He rides west, toward Asphodel," Torvold says behind me. I turn and his eyes dart down to the dagger in my hand. He blurts out, "How many of those do you have?"

"A few," I reply. I look down at the little White Witch clutching Torvold's hand. "Are you injured?" I ask her.

She touches the cut on her neck. "It stings," she says.

"But I'm already recovered."

"I have bandages in my saddle bag, your grace," Torvold tells the little girl. "Let us rejoin the others."

As I pass through the clearing, I start gathering up all my blades and hiding them in my dress. The White Witch runs to aid her minstrel friends, telling them that they've been rescued.

"Why did you go ahead of us like that?" Torvold asks behind me.

I don't look at him. I retrieve the knife that Gingivitis took from the littlest Witch. "I wanted to enjoy the fresh air," I reply, turning away from Torvold so I can put it in my bodice.

"Enjoy the—" he begins but cuts off when I stride to where I dropped the dagger in the leaflitter. "You must stay with the group, Princess."

I find it, stand, and walk away from him. I head toward the trees. I left a blade in Bear Trap's ear. After a moment Torvold catches up to me. He walks backward facing me for a moment, trying to get me to look at him.

"It was very dangerous. You could have been killed," he says. I brush past him, but he follows me. "You could have gotten Fortitude killed." He's getting angry now.

I go to where I see two bloody heaps and stop. Torvold steps in front of me.

"Princess, you must promise me you won't do something like that again," he demands. He makes a frustrated sound. "I was worried about you. When I heard screaming up the road, and you were gone—" he looks away and swallows, unable to finish. He reaches out to touch my arm.

This, right here. This standing close together in the soft light of sunset with his vulnerable eyes looking down on me as he reaches out with his lips parted like he's just about to kiss me. *This* is exactly what I can't do anymore. This is the kind of malarkey that's going to get me stuck in this rotten book forever. Or worse.

I take a step back and then around him, dodging his hand. "Fear not, good Sir Knight," I say cheerfully. "I was lost in thought and traveled too far ahead. I realized my folly as soon as I encountered danger, yet I knew that a simple band of ruffians would be no match for you. You have proven your valor yet again."

I go to Bear Trap and see that his head is no longer employed by the rest of his body. I seriously consider abandoning my blade but know I shouldn't. I find his head and keep my eyes averted as I yank out the dagger. I clean it hastily on the ground, trying not to barf.

Torvold has been silent. I look up at him and wish I didn't. Though my words have been nothing but praise, he looks as though I've slapped him.

"Is that all you have to say to me, my princess?" Torvold asks.

I straighten. I shift from foot to foot. I can't bear to see him hurt. "I'm sorry I scared you," I reply contritely.

"Why did you go ahead like that?" he asks again. "Did

I do something to offend you?" He takes a step closer. "Dex mentioned that you seemed angry I had spoken to our hostess alone, and that I wasn't forthcoming about it. I assure you, princess, all we did was speak."

Put that way, my behavior seems silly now. Of course, all they did was speak. I smile at my own foolishness, my face suddenly hot. He smiles when I do and moves closer to me.

"Was that it?" he asks, not letting it go until I answer him.

"Possibly," I admit stiffly. His smile broadens until his dimple makes an appearance. He's standing close to me again. Now he's touching my arm and drawing me against him. My hands come up to rest on his firm chest. Didn't I just say that I wasn't going to do this anymore?

"Are you going to kiss her?" asks a piping voice.

Torvold and I jump apart and see the little White Witch standing not far off with her minstrel friends. They have these half-embarrassed, half-expectant looks on their faces that tell me all of them have been watching us for a while. I practically run away to find Dex and Tudie.

I can't get jealous again. He's not mine. I can't get distracted by his shoulders and the dimple and the deep sweetness of his laugh. This is ridiculous. He's a *character*. In a *book*. From now on, no more playing footsie with Torvold.

I know I've said that a few times before, but this time I mean it.

9
HE'S PRETTY, BUT HE'S GOT AN ATTITUDE

We have to camp at the clearing because it's too late for us to move down the road unless we want to travel in the dark, which is never a good idea.

It gets really dark at night here. Like, can't see your hand in front of your face dark. Plus, we have to at least try to bury the bodies. The minstrels have shovels (I don't ask why) and the more able-bodied of us take turns digging.

There are ten members of this troupe, seven men and three women. From what I can gather they are all loosely related either by blood or marriage. And in some cases, both. Which is a little disturbing, to be honest.

I'm digging alongside the redheaded guy, who's named Vanil. He's in his mid-twenties, but he looks fifteen.

"How fares your cousin?" I ask, referring to the guy who got the lute broken over his head.

"Bashan?" he asks. I shrug and nod, not knowing his

name. "Oh, he's not my cousin, he's my uncle." Vanil thinks about it. "Well, I suppose he's also my cousin, but I call him uncle on account of he's married to my aunt, Gertie."

Vanil points out a round woman who is maybe thirty. I begin to wonder how a woman could be the aunt of someone only a few years her junior but stop myself before it gets too upsetting.

"He'll heal up in a trice," Vanil says, winking at me. "And I'm feeling much better, too, by the way."

I think he's flirting. I go back to digging. "I'm so pleased all of your troupe will recover from this dreadful encounter."

A thought suddenly occurs to him. "Oh no," he says, dropping his shovel. "We forgot about Rancor."

I climb out of my hole and follow him. "Is there a member of your party missing?" I ask urgently.

"Bloody hell," Vanil says, looking around at the near darkness. He finds a coil of rope and throws it over his shoulder. "We can't let him run around. It's not safe."

"I'll help you find him," I say.

Vanil looks at me like I'm crazy, then changes his mind. "Yes, you'd make perfect bait," he says, grabbing my hand and dragging me along with him.

"Pardon, but did you say bait?" I ask.

"You have nothing to fear, milady. For you, he will be as gentle as a lamb." Vanil thinks about it. "But watch out. He might try to stick you."

"I really don't think —," I begin, but Vanil interrupts with a sharp taxi-cab-hailing whistle.

"I'll just tie you to this tree," he says casually.

"What?" I say, jerking my hand out of his.

"It's just pretend," Vanil says. He throws the rope around me and the tree trunk. "I won't even knot it. You just stand there." He makes that sharp whistle again and runs away.

I could just walk away. I'm not actually tied here, but now I'm curious about Rancor. From the way Vanil was speaking of him, I'm picturing Sloth from *Goonies*.

I hear movement. Then heavy breathing. Okay, this was a dumb idea.

"Hello?" I call out into the dark.

Something white flashes off to my left and I turn. I'm looking to make a hasty escape when a unicorn prances right in front of me and stops. He shakes his head, his nostrils flaring.

Rancor is pure white like Thunder, and he has the same flowing mane and tail, but he's much smaller and more elegantly built. And of course, there's a horn sticking out of his head. It's a spiral, swirled with a sparkling crystal, like a dual-flavored soft serve ice cream, except instead of chocolate and vanilla it's made of ivory and diamond. He does a few passes in front of me and then he approaches.

The sharp tip of his long, spiral horn comes dangerously close to my face while he sniffs me. He whinnies and bares his teeth. For a moment I'm positive this bugger is going to bite me. I can tell he's thinking about it. But instead, he catches the rope between his teeth and pulls it off.

"Thank you," I say. He whinnies again. "Can I touch you, or am I going to get gored if I try?"

He drops his head. I pat it. That goes okay, so I give him a little rub behind the ears, too. He sniffs my palm and licks it.

"You want some salt?" I ask him. He sneezes. "I'll get you some salt." I start to walk away with Rancor trailing behind like a leashed puppy.

Vanil rushes toward me with a scared look on his face. "Are you *uninjured*, princess?" he asks.

"Just fine, thank you," I reply.

The unicorn follows me back to the clearing, where I've left my pack with Tudie. Everyone freezes when they see us. Torvold holds up a hand and rises from the ground slowly.

"Princess, don't make any sudden movements," Torvold says. "When I tell you, dive to the left as fast as you can."

"Why?" I ask, shrugging.

"There's a unicorn behind you."

I laugh. "I know." I turn and gesture for Rancor to keep coming.

He follows me right to where Dex and Tudie are backing away in horror. Everyone is backing away in horror. I pick up my salt pouch, shake a little into the palm of my hand, and hold it out. Rancor licks my hand over and over. When the salt is gone, he *thinks* about biting it.

"That's enough of that," I tell him. We look each other in the eye. He sneezes again. I scratch his ears, looking around at everyone. "He's a little nippy, but we'll get past it," I tell them.

"A little nippy?" Vanil pulls the neck of his jerkin aside to show a big white semi-circle of scars over his shoulder. I bet if I were closer, I could see the individual tooth marks. "He did that to me once when I was feeding him."

"Never turn your back on a unicorn," Bashan says. He lifts his jerkin to show me what is most likely a gore hole from a unicorn horn in his side. "That's what you get if you do."

"Why do you keep him?" Jackanet asks, dumbfounded.

The minstrels share a look. "They're lucky," Gertie replies like it's obvious.

I look at Rancor. "No one understands you, do they?" I coo. Rancor knickers. I pet his soft nose. "Where do you want to sleep tonight?" I ask him.

He turns and clip-clops away. I follow him to a nice spot over by one of the wagons.

"I'll brush you in the morning and bring you some more salt," I promise. He nudges me, eyes closing, and I go away so he can get some sleep.

I go back to the clearing, get handed a bowl of stew, and seat myself next to the little White Witch.

"I want to ask your name but every time I do that lately I get stonewalled," I tell her.

She doesn't give me a hint one way or the other.

"Fine. I'm just going to ask, then. What Virtue are you?"

"Something you have lost," she tells me, frowning down at her stew.

"Patience?" I guess dryly.

She smiles and shakes her head. "Faith."

Not going to lie. That stings a little. "How am I supposed to have Faith when I know —," I glance over at Torvold, chatting pleasantly with Vanil, "when I *know* the story doesn't end well?"

She looks into my eyes, seeming much older than me. Actually, she seems much older than anyone. Ever.

"What is Faith to you?" she asks in return. "Do you think it's believing something will work out when you already know it does?"

"No," I reply. "But I don't think it's the opposite of that, either."

She glances over at Torvold. "Jump," she says. "And the net will appear."

There's a unicorn nibbling on my head.

He's not technically biting me, but he is letting me

know that if I don't get up and fetch him some salt, toothy things are going to happen.

I have twelve days left.

I rise and stretch. Rancor whickers at me. I pull out some salt and let him lick my hand until it's soggy. I feel gross. Like, full body nasty, and it's about to get nastier. This is another thing no one mentions in epic fantasy books. Right now I've got to find a nice spot to dig a hole, so I can poop in it. That makes me feel super princess-y.

Rancor comes with me. At least I know no one will walk up on me accidentally because everyone stays as far away from Rancor as they can.

When I rejoin the group, there is a discussion in progress about the road ahead. It's not clear yet who is going with whom.

Everyone wants Torvold to go with them. Torvold, however, thinks it would be best if we split up.

"My path is long and treacherous," Torvold is saying.

"Not if you were to come to the city with us," Bashan replies logically. "It's just up the road a pace."

Torvold frowns. "No, you don't understand. I must protect the Virtues," he says.

"What? Everybody's?" Gertie guffaws. "You must be popular at parties."

Torvold is momentarily speechless.

"Sir Torvold the Bold is on a quest," Jackanet announces grandly. "He cannot escort you to the city."

"How do you know his quest doesn't lead to the city?" Vanil asks.

"Lots of virtues in the city," Gertie adds. "Course, most of them are for sale."

Faith tugs on Torvold's arm, and he bends down so she can whisper in his ear. "Really?" he asks doubtfully. Faith nods. "All right then," Torvold says, turning to the minstrels. "I will accompany you to the city."

The minstrels look very relieved.

"Sure, you can tag along with us," Vanil says. Bashan gives him a look. "What?" Vanil says.

"Gather your things, everyone. We're off to Market Town!" Bashan announces.

For all the fanfare, it's actually rather a long way to Market Town. There are plenty of places to sit in the carriages, and now that nine mounts have found themselves bandit-less, there are also plenty of horses to ride.

But I have to walk.

Rancor won't let me or my salt get more than a few paces away from him and no one will get more than ten paces within Rancor. The other horses are terrified of him, too.

Torvold has been busying himself all morning making sure that the White Witches are no longer wearing white but are disguised in costumes supplied by the minstrels. I don't want to ask Tudie or Dex and insult them, but I'm wondering why when Asphodel put out his *fatwa* on

White Witches, not one of them thought it might be a good day to try, say, yellow.

Once we're on our way, Torvold rides to the end of our merry little parade (where I am) with a stormy look on his face.

"Why are you on foot, princess?" he asks me.

I point my thumb back at Rancor, my face stiff with annoyance.

Torvold chuckles. "Why aren't you riding him then?"

Rancor and I share a look, and I shake my head. "We're not ready for that."

I cough. It's hard to breathe, what with all the hooves and wagon wheels kicking up dust in front of me. I blow a pebble from between my lips. Torvold's shoulders are shaking with quiet laughter.

"I wish I could ride," I say, hoping to make the unicorn feel guilty. "It's very gritty back here."

Torvold wheels Thunder around and reaches his hand down. "Climb up," he tells me. Rancor paws the ground and tosses his head, but Thunder is not afraid of him.

I know I shouldn't. I should just trudge along back here with my antisocial mythical beast, eating road dirt and getting blisters. But instead, I take Torvold's hand and he pulls me up. I sit in front of him, with his arms on either side of me so he can hold the reins. Rancor trots up and tries to bite Torvold, but Thunder won't have any of that. He faces Rancor and goes right at him. Rancor backs off, but not that far. He looks at me and sneezes.

"I'm right here, you big baby," I tell Rancor. He whickers at me and settles in next to Thunder, acting docile, but probably plotting his revenge.

I forgot how comfortable it was to lean back against Torvold. Even with the chainmail on. I'm not getting all hot and bothered, I'm just noticing basic bodily topography. It just so happens that where I dip, he swells.

That didn't come out right.

"You are quiet, my princess," Torvold says. The side of his face brushes against mine as he tries to curve around me and see my expression.

As a conversation starter, that one stinks. What is anyone supposed to do with that? If I had something that I thought I could say out loud, I would. The problem is, in my head, where the commentary is usually PG, everything is starting to sound R-rated, and this isn't that kind of book.

"Have you been to the city before?" I ask, figuring my best bet is to change the subject.

"Many times," Torvold replies. "I was born in a city."

"Me too," I answer honestly. "But I've been away from people for a while."

"Did your handmaidens accompany you to the tower?"

I think about my friends back in Los Angeles and how I had to leave them when I moved. I didn't even bother to try and make friends in Fresno, or even raise my eyes from the floor long enough to see other faces in the hallways, for that matter. I knew I'd be graduating and leaving them soon, too. I gave up on even trying to be happy, I guess.

"No. I've been alone this whole time."

He's silent for a while. "That must have been difficult."

"I could have made it easier on myself. I could have had companions, but I was angry," I admit. I drop my head. "I've made a lot of mistakes."

"It seems to me, princess, that many things have occurred that have been out of your hands." He curves around me again to see my expression. "I, too, would be angry if I had to leave my home and go to a place that is much like a prison, all because of other people's desires."

I meet his eyes. Look, I know he's talking about Princess Pleasant. I haven't totally lost my mind yet. But everything he's saying fits me. Like he fits me. I look away, trying not to cry. This is not a crying moment. He's a great guy who thinks I'm someone I'm not. Also, a little perspective is in order. I moved to Fresno. I did not get locked in a tower. Well, not until I locked myself in one, that is.

"Thank you," I say when my voice is steady again.

"Why do you thank me?"

"For your compassion. It's been a long time since anyone has tried to understand me."

He brushes his cheek against my hair. "I want to understand everything about you," he says softly.

Why did I get on his horse? Could I get any dumber?

I'm trying to think up any reason to get down. I even consider telling him I've got a record-breaking case of hemorrhoids and I'm better off walking when we notice a disturbance at the front end of our merry band of misfits. Torvold wraps one arm more tightly around my waist and kicks Thunder into a cantor.

When we get to the front of our party, Jackanet is holding up the piece of parchment with the map on it, turning it over, and Dex is glaring at him with her fists on her hips.

"Obviously, this isn't on the map," Jackanet grouses.

"Maybe if you turn the map upside down one more time it will suddenly make sense to you," she says sarcastically.

"What the matter?" Torvold asks as we nose Thunder close to the huddle.

"It's the road, milord," Bashan says, peering down at the ground with his hat twirling about in his hands anxiously.

"What do you mean?" Torvold asks, moving forward until we can both see what everyone is arguing about. There is a giant crack in the ground.

"It's gone," Tudie says.

10
PHILL MCKRACKEN

The crack is about fifteen feet wide. Which may not seem like an impossible distance to jump, and in movies, heroes go soaring over rooftops and jumping distances that are much wider than fifteen feet. But trust me, when you see it for real, fifteen feet is way too far to jump.

And it's not like there are any handy trees about that we can chop down and turn into a makeshift bridge, either. And even if there were, fifteen feet is still too far to consider putting down a few rickety planks in order to trundle across with all the horses, wagons, and gear. I would think twice about even *walking* across a plank that spanned fifteen feet with no handrail over what seems to be an endless abyss, let alone ride over it on horseback.

"It can't go on forever," Torvold says, looking left and right along the rift. "Maybe we can go around it."

That prospect does not appeal much, either, because, on each side of the road, there is now a smelly swamp. There wasn't a smelly swamp fifty yards back. This new, unfortunate terrain came out of nowhere, but that's somewhat common in Lucitopia. It's my theory that the abrupt scenery changes happen because the author thinks action to action and she doesn't like to spend too much time writing about a bunch of boring transitional places. She thinks in jump cuts, or like one of those wipes that you see in Star Wars movies where a line goes across the screen and the intrepid heroes are suddenly at their destination of Mos Eisley or whatever.

"I don't remember any bogs on the way to Market Town," Bashan mutters, taking the map away from Jackanet. "None of this is supposed to be here," he announces after he glares at the hand-drawn pictures.

I look back over my shoulder at Torvold. "It's probably enchanted," I say, and he nods in agreement.

"It's a test, then. I get these a lot," he replies.

"Really?" I ask, intrigued. "Is that because you're a knight?"

He shrugs and continues to peer into the distance. "Left, or right?" he asks me.

Honestly, they both look like bad choices. "Right?" I guess, just to pick a direction. Torvold turns Thunder's head to the right, and Rancor runs to cut us off. The maniac stands in front of Thunder, shaking his head and stamping his front hoof. I glance over my shoulder again to see Torvold smiling back at me with a raised eyebrow. "How about left, then?" I suggest.

Rancor sneezes in agreement.

"Left it is," Torvold says, turning Thunder again. "We'll scout ahead and try to find a way around," he informs Jackanet.

"Would you like me to accompany you?" Jackanet adds, narrowing his eyes at me distrustfully. Like I'm going to drown Torvold in the bog or something. Sheesh.

"We won't be long," Torvold replies, declining. "Keep the White Witches in the cart and out of sight as best as you can. In case anyone comes by," he adds quietly.

Jackanet nods solemnly in reply. "We are merely humble players, sir, on our way to Market Town," the squire says, overacting horribly as he doffs his hat.

"Good," Torvold replies, satisfied that this deception should keep them safe enough. And that Jackanet's acting is bad enough that no one will ask for an impromptu performance.

Rancor steps off the road and enters the bog first. He whinnies and rolls his eyes when his dainty hooves meet the muck, but he doesn't stop or allow Thunder to go past him. He actually nips at the larger warhorse to keep him from coming abreast. Rancor begins fastidiously picking his way through the squelchy ground, finding the driest route, and Thunder follows.

"What kind of trials have you faced before, Sir Torvold?" I ask.

I feel him huff a laugh, remembering. “They usually have something to do with testing my character.”

When he doesn’t continue, I twist my head around to see him suppressing an embarrassed smile. “How so?” I press, and he squirms some more.

“Nothing I care to speak of specifically, but they have each tested different qualities that are required in a knight.”

“Like?”

He repositions me in front of him, more internally uncomfortable than externally. He’s trying to get me to look forward so I can’t read his expression.

“Courtesy,” he begins.

“Which you easily passed,” I say. “And?”

“Generosity.”

I blow air between my lips in a *pshaw* sound. “Passed,” I declare, making him laugh sheepishly. “Next?”

“Humility.”

“*...he says as he blushes humbly,*” I narrate. “And?”

“Piety.”

I turn my head to meet his eyes. “Are you pious?” I wasn’t raised religious at all, but I’ve always been curious about it.

Torvold nods. “I am. In my own way. My parents are very traditional. I see things differently than they do, but I still believe in god.”

I study him for a moment, watching a slight furrow crease his brow and then disappear as he thinks about something complicated and mildly troubling. Torvold is not one of the silent types who make you wonder if there's anyone home. He's one of the silent types who is quiet because his thoughts are moving so fast there's no way his mouth could keep up with them. I really, really like that. I like it *too* much. I could watch this guy think all day.

I make myself face forward. "So that's courtesy, generosity, humility, and piety," I list. "Anything else?"

"Why do you ask?" He's deflecting now.

"I want to know what qualities are left so I can guess what type of test we might be facing," I reply, but that's just an excuse. This is torturing him for some reason, and I'm loving it. I wonder what he's trying so hard *not* to say.

He chuckles under his breath. "There is one more, but that's been sort of an ongoing test since I met you."

"Patience?" I guess, and he laughs outright.

"It *does* require patience," he says, and I can feel his body heating up. He's so embarrassed right now he's about to burst into flames. It's so adorable I can't resist squirming closer to him.

"Tell me," I urge.

He lets out a conflicted sigh. "Well—" he begins, but he doesn't get the chance to finish.

Rancor suddenly bolts into the mist, whinnying like a psycho. I feel Torvold pull me tighter against him and kick Thunder into a trot under us. We splash through puddles and swirls of fog that seem to get denser, until the veils of smoke and mist suddenly part and we see a tree.

Rancor is prancing around the base of the tree in a circle, tossing his head and baring his teeth as he snaps at the air. It's like he's trying to bite at a swarm of flies around him, but I don't see any insects. Crazy unicorn.

Thunder comes to a halt and Torvold and I look up at the branches of the tree. The knobbles and knots of the leafless tree's branches form unmistakable shapes. Inlayed in the bark are faces, torsos, and outstretched arms.

"Those are people," I say, my tone made flat by shock. The bark-people's frozen expressions range from surprised to angry to absolutely horrified.

"It's like they're trying to claw their way out of the tree," Torvold adds in a hushed tone. I feel him lean slightly forward as he peers at the shapes in the bark. "Edrick," he whispers.

I turn in the saddle to look at Torvold's stark expression. "You know him." It's a statement, not a question, but Torvold nods in reply anyway.

"He's a knight."

"He *was* a knight, sir Torvold the Bold," says another, eldritch-sounding voice. "Now, he is a prisoner of the oak."

Rancor finally stops his crazed circling of the trunk and comes to a stop between us and a very old man in a hooded cloak who is leaning heavily on a wooden staff.

"Mage Phillip. You've gone too far," Torvold says. He's angry, and not just to mask his fear. "Set them free!"

"I did not imprison these knights, nor can I help them

escape," the old man says, staring up into the branches that are really reaching arms and elongated fingers. "It was Asphodel who imprisoned them here when they would not give their souls to him, and it is you who must set them free by killing Asphodel."

I feel Torvold tensing up behind me.

"I swore to another duty, given to me by the Knight's Council," he says, nearly strangling on the words in his frustration. "I cannot abandon my duty and keep my honor."

"Your honor is the least of what's at stake if you don't kill Asphodel!" the little guy says with a quivering voice.

Well, that's just not fair. Torvold obviously wants to fight Asphodel, but the Council told him otherwise. It's not his fault he's stuck out here in the sticks, babysitting a drama club and a bunch of White Witches, but he won't make excuses for himself. He's too honorable to defend his own honor.

"I'm sorry, but who are you again?" I ask. "Are you some kind of sorcerer?"

He gasps, affronted. "I am no such thing! I am his majesty's magician, Phillip the Beige!"

Beige. A snarf of laughter escapes me. I feel Torvold's breath huff the back of my hair. I think he's trying not to laugh as well, and that wrecks it for me. He and I are trading snickers, egged on by the other, but we manage to pull it together while Phillip the Beige looks increasingly put out, and not just by our irreverence. Rancor keeps doing these little fly-bys where he trots in, tries to bite the magician, and then trots off again.

"You would know me better, Princess Pleasant, if you had been at court with your father this past year," he says huffily, trying to keep his dignity while trying to avoid a nippy unicorn. "I am a great magician!"

"Okay, sure. But as a magician, why aren't you facing off against Asphodel?" I ask. "Why don't *you* go kill him?"

Phillip the Beige's wrinkled face goes nearly smooth with fear. "He'd kill me."

What a punk.

"Uh-huh," I say. "So, you, a great magician, expect Torvold, a knight with no magic, to go face off *against a sorcerer*? And you're going to stand here and do what, exactly?"

Rancor nibbles on Phillip's hem and he has to wheel around to swat him away. "I guard the prisoners of the oak," he says, irritated and doubling down on his self-importance in the face of such disrespect.

"It's a bit late for guarding them, don't you think? They're already *bark*. How much worse can it get for them, really?"

Phillip clutches his staff and regards me sulkily. "You're a right harridan, you are. You should go back to your tower."

That does it. I'm about to get down off this horse and kick him in the cassock, but, laughing, Torvold holds me tighter and won't let me. I can tell he's enjoying this.

"It serves Asphodel if we argue amongst ourselves," he reminds both of us, then he changes the subject. "How do we get across the rift, Good Phillip the Beige?"

He added the 'good' bit to do a little butt kissing. It works, too. Phil perks up.

"Answer me these questions three," he says, waving his hands about and making the long sleeves on his cloak flap impressively.

Really? What a rip-off. That's from *Monty Python and the Holy Grail.* I roll my eyes and mumble, "Waste of time," under my breath.

"Stop it," Torvold whispers in my ear, but he's trying not to laugh again, and I know he agrees with me. "What are your questions, O Phillip the Beige?"

"Wait, what happens if we answer incorrectly?" I interject.

Phillip had opened his mouth to ask the first question and he shuts it again, looking annoyed. "You don't get across."

He opens his mouth again but I interrupt again.

"And then what?"

"Well, you stay here."

"And where is Asphodel? Is he on *this* side of the rift?"

"Ah—no," Phillip says, a hint of doubt creeping into his tone.

"Then who will kill Asphodel if Torvold is stuck here?" I persist. The Beige One looks a little scared now. He drops his arms.

"He's got to answer the questions!" he blathers.

"Why?"

"To test his character." He sniffs and looks anywhere but at me.

"I have only had the pleasure of Sir Torvold's company for a short while, but I can already say that his character is beyond reproach. You can take my word for it. I'm a princess. We know about these things."

"But—"

"And anyway, who else have you got?" I wave a hand at the prisoners in the oak. "It's not like *they're* going to be able to kill Asphodel. Quite simply, you've run out of knights."

Phillip the Beige sputters at me before lamenting, "This is not how it's done!"

"I'm aware of that, but consider this. On the off chance that we fail your test, what happens then? Sir Torvold is stuck here, unable to even *get* to Asphodel let alone kill him, and this entire kingdom will be lost. Is that something you want?" He pauses, thinking it over. "Just let us pass," I say, rolling my eyes. "We won't tell anyone."

He looks between the two of us warily. "It's not the sort of thing I can have getting around."

"You have our word," Torvold says. When I glance back at him, he's watching me with an amused look on his face.

The magician thinks about it for a few more seconds,

but we both know which way this is going to go. Phillip the Beige may be kind of a boob, but he's not an idiot.

"Fine! You may go. And take this insufferable unicorn!" he says, taking another swipe at Rancor who has crept up on the magician and tried to nibble his head. Phillip the Beige waves his arms in a very spell-casting type gesture, then he, the swamp, the rift, the tree, and the fog, all disappear.

11
PIG IN A BLANKET

We appear in a forest. Thunder is still under us, and Rancor is still prancing around in agitated circles, but the rift in the ground is gone. We look around.

"Any idea where we are?" I ask Torvold.

"No," he replies. "Can you hear our party?"

I stop and listen, then shake my head when all I hear is Rancor's annoyed whickering.

"I have to admit, I'm a bit turned around," Torvold says.

Rancor stops, looks at me, and sneezes. "Which way?" I ask him. He shakes his mane, almost like he's saying no, and then stares at me, pointedly not moving.

"I think he's lost, too," I say, looking back at Torvold over my shoulder. I chuckle, realizing something. "And apparently, I've learned how to speak Unicorn."

Torvold chuckles with me, both of us smiling at the

other. Then his smile falters, and his gaze drops from my eyes to my mouth. He's gone completely still. I hold my breath, even though I suddenly need buckets of oxygen. Wait. Is he about to kiss me? Worse. I really want him to kiss me. I turn away from his nearing lips and face front, convinced he can hear my heart throbbing for him. This is ridiculous. He's not a real person. He's a character in a book. Why do I have to keep reminding myself of that fact?

"Which way do you think is best?" I say, just to say something.

"We're losing the light," he replies, his voice low and unsteady.

"Should we wait until morning to search for the others?"

"That might be best," he says. "Here, I'll help you down."

Sure, he feels real. Alarmingly real. His hands on my waist, as he helps me down from Thunder, are solid and trustworthy. His shoulders and biceps bunch in a convincing way as he takes my weight and lowers me to the ground, and the closed-off look that has shuttered his usually inviting brown eyes convey something that seems to be genuine hurt. All of this signals that I have refused the kiss of what appears to be an actual person and not a storybook knight. But he's *not* real. He's just really well-written.

Torvold turns away from me as soon as I'm on my feet

again, his eyes on the ground. I shift from foot to foot, knowing that I've wounded him, but I don't know what to say to make it better. I find myself following him, and reaching out to touch his arm anyway.

"I didn't mean to—" I begin.

"No, please don't explain. You shouldn't have to, Princess," he says, shaking his head, and looking like he'd give anything for a do-over. "I apologize for my behavior. You have no chaperone, and if you feel I've taken advantage of you in any way—"

"You haven't," I interrupt quickly. "And it's not that I don't—"

When I stop, he pins me with a look. "Don't what?" he asks, cautiously hopeful.

I can't say anything that will encourage him. That would be cruel. "I can't tell you how much I value your regard," I say.

He breathes out a pained laugh, like I just punched him in the stomach.

"What I mean is, I feel perfectly safe with you," I try again. Why am I still talking? Luckily, he doesn't let me make it any worse.

"I understand your meaning plainly enough," he says. He composes himself and stands up straighter. "If you'd care to unsaddle Thunder while I gather some firewood, we could settle in twice as fast."

When I give him a brisk nod, he departs.

What the heck is going on? And why is "heck" the

only modifier coming to mind? For the thousandth time, I wish Lucitopia would let me use stronger language, but it won't, not even in my own head.

I think things like *phooey* and *darn it* while I unsaddle Thunder, and give him a good brushing. I try to do the same for Rancor but he's still worked up about something. His hide twitches under my hands, and I only get in one or two strokes before Rancor trots away.

I clear a space, trying to set up the best camp I can, but we left most of our stuff with the group. Torvold has been gone for quite some time. I rub my arms against the cold, trying hard not to remember how warm he is, or how comfortably his arms fit around me. I'm pacing. The sun has set, and it is fully dark now. I hear the undergrowth rustling, and a snap as if someone had stepped on a branch. I spin to face the sound, my senses straining into the impenetrable darkness.

"Sir Torvold?" I call. My voice sounds scared, even to me. "Rancor?" I try again, this time with a little less quaver. No answer. I pull out one of my knives.

Okay, when I'm watching a horror movie, the last thing I want the girl to do is to go into the darkness to find out what made that suspicious noise. The *second* to last thing I want her to do is to stay put, though. Think about it. This would usually be the part where we cut to the killer's point of view as they creep up on the petrified girl who's standing there with her arms wrapped around herself, calling out for someone who's already been murdered. Well, not in my movie, sister. If I see anything out there that isn't either Torvold or Rancor, I'm going to stab first and ask questions later.

I hear more movement in the underbrush and then the sound of low, grumbly voices. As I get closer, the voices get louder and I see the glow of a fire. Those aren't human shadows or human voices. A few more steps, and I know what they are. Ogres.

I think they might be arguing about something. Or maybe their language always includes a lot of shoving. I don't know their culture. I take a chance and venture closer because I see something on the ground by the fire. It's a wriggling bundle. I ease through the bushes, listening to the ogres grunting and snarling at each other with a sinking feeling in my stomach. That bundle looks familiar. I get near enough to see through the ogres' moving legs as they jostle each other around the fire.

They've got Torvold.

A thick rope is wound around him from shoulders to knees. He sort of looks like a cocktail wiener wrapped up in pastry, which is inherently funny, but I don't feel like laughing. I can see him struggling, trying to inch his way out of the wound rope, but at least he doesn't look like he's panicking or anything. That's a relief.

Meanwhile, the ogres are nearly coming to blows above him. I turn my attention to their conversation.

Now, I'm going to skip right over all the descriptive

turns of phrases that include words like "thug" and "brute" or even "dim-witted" because quite honestly, that feels a little racist to me. I mean, sure, they're ogres. They're ten feet tall, green, muscles like boulders, and they've got lower mandible tusks that encumber their speech, making big words unintelligible. Their clothing choices tend toward the furry loin cloth and leather department, but just because a species is physically endowed and has no fashion sense, does not necessarily mean that they are any less mentally competent than the next mythical creature. Yes, they grunt a lot. Maybe their syntax isn't so great. But I'm going to keep the commentary on their intelligence to myself from here on out.

"He a knight. We bring him," says the ogre with his hair pulled up into a high ponytail by a fetching, spike-studded iron band.

"No, he different!" insists another ogre, this one has his septum pierced. "No, bring. He kill sorcerer for us!"

Torvold flops around, nodding and trying to shout at them around his gag. Obviously, he's more than willing to go kill Asphodel if they will set him free.

"Asphodel want all knights!" Ponytail says, emphasizing his point by shoving Septum and nearly knocking him down.

The third ogre, the one without any superficial markers that I can see so I'll just think of him as Boring, finally stands up and gets between Ponytail and Septum.

"We eat," Boring decides. Maybe I was a little hasty

assigning a name. Eating Torvold is not boring. Bloodthirsty or Hungry might have been more suitable.

"Not eat. *Asphodel*," Ponytail insists. "He give gold."

The word gold caught their attention, but Boring still looks like he cares more about food than money. It's a three-way tie, apparently, and that might keep them busy long enough for me to come up with a plan.

Except we all know that's not true. I never come up with a plan.

"Shh!" Septum says. The ogres stop and listen intently to the darkness outside the circle of light created by their fire.

Oh no, have they heard me somehow? I try to sink into the underbrush as best as I can, but soon realize it's not me they're listening for.

I hear rustling on the other side of the ogre's campsite. The ogres jump and whirl around toward the sound, behaving as if they're petrified. I wonder what could possibly scare an ogre, but I very much do not want to find out at this moment.

The ogres' watchfulness is finally interrupted by the sound of one of their stomachs growling. Boring looks down at his belly. "We eat," he decides, indicating Torvold.

I don't think this through at all. I just jump out of the bushes and into the light of the fire with my knife hidden behind my back.

"If it's gold you want, I will give it to you. Release my knight," demands my mouth, much to the surprise of the rest of me. From whence will this gold I keep promising come? So far, I've promised it to every bandit-slash-ogre I've encountered without ever having had any gold on my person. "You will be rewarded handsomely," I continue to lie.

There is a long, awkward pause. Then the ogres crack up laughing. Torvold wasn't panicking before I got here, but he is now. I maybe, probably, most likely—okay, *definitely*—miscalculated. Nothing I can do about it now, though. I'll just have to keep going.

"With gold, you could buy lots of food. Far more than you can get out of him," I say with a desultory gesture in Torvold's direction.

"Grab her," Boring says in an offhand way. "Eat her too."

Rats.

Ponytail comes to get me. I throw the knife I've got hidden behind my back right between his eyes. It lands and sinks in, but it does not have the effect I was going for. The ogre stops, crosses his eyes to look at the hilt, grabs it, and yanks it out.

He looks at me. "Hey," he says, sounding offended. "That hurt."

Torvold is flopping around like a fish at the bottom of a boat, screaming something around his gag that I can't make out. It sounds like "Art". Why is he talking about... oh, I get it. I pull another blade out of my sleeve and throw it at the ogre's *heart* because apparently their heads are not vital. And I refuse to comment on that blatantly human-species-biased world-building.

Ponytail stops, looks down, and goes to pull this second blade out as he did the first, but instead, he falls forward, either dead or well on his way to it.

Right about now Septum and Boring have caught wise to the fact that I am not, in fact, helpless, and they pick up a club and an ax respectively before stalking toward me. I throw another knife, and Boring knocks it away in midair. Then he gives me a look. It's a look I've never seen before, but I know what it means, and my knees go weak. They aren't going to tie me up and bring me to Asphodel, I realize. They are going to kill me and probably eat me. I think this is the first time I've ever been truly afraid for my life in Lucitopia.

Whatever shock or disbelief was keeping my fear at bay decides now is the time to desert me. I scrabble with my skirt, gathering it up in one hand and reaching beneath it to get to the knife in my garter with the other. I get my knife out and hold it up, panting and scared out of my mind. I don't even think I can run, I'm so petrified. My legs feel frozen to the spot.

But instead of killing me with one blow, the ogres pull up short, turn, and run away.

I have no idea what just happened, but I don't care. I've been trapped in this fairy tale long enough to know better than to just stand around. I rush to Torvold, drop down on my knees next to him, and pull off his gag.

"Are you injured?" I ask. My hands feel numb and like they don't belong to me. I can barely keep ahold of my knife as I start cutting his bonds.

"I'm unharmed," he says, grunting a little around the tightness of the rope. He probably hasn't been able to take a full breath since they tied him up. "You?" he asks.

"I am uninjured," I say, but my whole body is visibly shaking now.

Torvold shrugs off the last of the rope and I don't know if it's him or me who instigates it, but as soon as he's free I'm in his arms and getting what is probably the best hug of my life.

"So scared," I say into his chest, breathing in deep, calming lung-fulls of his scent.

"It's okay," he replies, his head resting comfortably on top of mine.

It takes a few more moments of being held for me to stop shaking. I really thought I was going to die.

"It's okay," he whispers the whole time.

He's smoothing my hair, kind of like he's petting me, which you'd think would be off-putting, but I can't tell you how soothing I find it. I've never been a pet before, but I understand now why it makes cats purr.

"You saved my life," he says.

"I didn't." I ease back, staying in the loose circle of his arms. "Something scared them off."

Torvold eyes something over my shoulder suspiciously and motions for me to turn around. Rancor is standing behind me, looking kind of dopey the way equines do when they're tired or relaxed.

"Thank you," I say to Rancor. He sneezes and wanders off. "Why is everyone so terrified of unicorns?" I ask Torvold.

Torvold chuckles and shrugs. "Everyone but you," he says, not even trying to explain it to me. "Can you stand?"

My first thought is *of course I can stand,* but then as Torvold helps me to my feet I realize how shaky my legs are. Near-death experiences are no joke.

"We should quit this place in case they return," he says, stepping away from me. He's giving me space, probably because I told him *I value your regard* and not *I want to make out with you immediately*. But I don't want space.

"May I hold your hand?" I ask, immediately regretting my wussy word choice. "It's just I—"

"Yes," he interrupts, not making me explain myself.

He takes my hand, picks Calx up off the ground as we pass it by, and brings me back to our camp.

12
UNICORN BEER RUN

I don't know when or how I fell asleep. We got back to camp and sat down on the ground, both of us too tired to collect firewood, and it seemed like the next second I woke up.

"Good morning," Torvold says. He's standing next to Thunder, adjusting the saddle's girth strap.

I mumble something in reply and pick some leaves out of my hair. My stomach reminds me that it's been a while since I've had a meal with an embarrassingly loud burble.

"Is there anything to eat?" I ask.

Torvold takes a small bundle of biscuits from his pack and hands them to me. "Mind your teeth," he warns, and rightly so.

I manage to gnaw an edge off of one of them, which I then have to let sit on my tongue, soaking up all the moisture in my mouth, in order to soften it enough to chew.

He watches me and then hands me his water skin. I take a big swig and wash the lump down.

"Mmm," I say, handing him back both the water and the rest of the "food". "Can't imagine why you've been hiding that in your pack this whole time."

"It's almost as delicious as chimera griff."

He and I both smile at that callback. He breaks eye contact first and studies his hands, which are idly fiddling with the clasp on one of his saddle bags. "We should be on our way. The rest of the group must be very worried about us."

"Where's Rancor?" I ask.

"Haven't seen him all morning," Torvold replies.

"How long have you been awake?"

He drops his eyes and shakes his head, refusing to answer. Then he helps me into the saddle, effectively changing the subject. I get the feeling that Torvold barely slept at all last night.

"You're going to have to sleep eventually, you know," I say as he takes his place behind me in the saddle.

"I will."

"When?"

"When you are safe, my princess," he replies.

I have no response to that. I want to tell him I can look after myself, and that I don't need someone to watch out for me while I sleep. In a forest. That is demonstrably full of ogres. But that is a big fat lie.

"Tonight, if we are still on our own, I will keep watch," I tell him.

He doesn't respond, but I do feel his arm tighten slightly around me before he seems to remember himself. He leans away from me. It makes me sad, but there's nothing I can do that will make it better. I have to let it go, forget about it, and about any possibility of being with him, even though that doesn't feel right. He and I feel right together.

It occurs to me that maybe Torvold isn't the one being tested here.

We ride out, but as the time passes with no road in sight, we both become increasingly alarmed.

"This is wrong," Torvold mutters, looking down at the ground. He pulls up on Thunder's reins and points into the leaf litter. "Those are our tracks." He looks around. "We're back to where we camped last night."

"Did we turn at all?" I ask because I have no idea.

Though I know broad strokes about trees, like the difference between a conifer from a deciduous, all of the big, old leafy trees here look pretty much the same to me. And it's not like a forest has many other defining features in it. I can't even see the sun in the sky the canopy is so thick.

"We haven't," he replies. Though I have no idea how he knows that, I trust his judgment. Which means that unless we went around the world, there is no way we could be back where we started.

"It's magic, then. An illusion of some kind," I say. "Do you feel like you were hit by a spell?"

He laughs ruefully. "Not in the way you mean."

He dismounts while I'm still trying to figure that out, and lifts his arms to help me down. Leaning out of the saddle with my hands planted on Torvold's shoulders, I see Rancor standing among the trees, watching us.

"What is he doing?" I ask.

Torvold puts me down before turning to study Rancor's odd behavior. "It looks like he's waiting for us."

Rancor huffs through his nose and stomps his forelegs impatiently. Then he makes a high whinny that is borderline disturbing, wheels around, and trots away into the thick fog gathering ominously behind him. Torvold and I share a look and, leading Thunder by the reins, we go after the cranky, white weirdo.

Rancor comes back for us several times, blowing air through his lips, sidling, and stamping his hooves to get us to hurry. We follow him until the mist parts, revealing what must be the most improbably placed castle ever.

Most fortifications are put atop a high hill or in the middle of a wide-open plain, someplace that gives the people inside the castle a panoramic view of any potential threats, while also providing a natural deterrent to invaders. Think about any castles you know of in the real world. They're either on cliffsides, on top of big hills, or they're in the middle of some kind of body of water.

But *this* castle is sitting in a forest. And it's white. And it looks brand new. I know I'm in a storybook, but this isn't normal. Torvold must get the same creeped-out feeling I do because as soon as the castle appears he stiffens and throws out an arm to stop me from advancing, immediately distrustful.

"That can't be real," he says.

"Certainly not," I agree with a grimace. Rancor turns back again, shakes his head, and then trots through the main gate.

"Are you sure Rancor doesn't want us dead?" Torvold asks.

I consider that. "Not entirely, but a goring is more his style. He'd want to see the light go out of our eyes," I decide.

"Fair point," Torvold agrees with a chuckle.

He starts to follow Rancor, and I grab his arm, stopping him. "Wait. All that mist. Maybe we wandered into the Land of the Fey?"

Torvold screws up his face like he thinks I'm crazy. "Fairies aren't *real*, Princess," he says, and we both enter the highly improbable and most likely magical castle, which better not have any beautiful, insane, and probably murderous fairies in it like all the popular books I've been reading lately, or I'm going to kill Torvold.

If the castle appeared to be deserted from the outside, the inside is anything but. Torvold and I are immediately plunged into what appears to be a Ren fair, that is completely devoid of gorgeous, backstabbing fairies. In fact, the most beautiful person here is Torvold, but I'd probably still think he was the most beautiful person here even if the place was crawling with fairies.

Throngs of perfectly normal people, who all appear to be quite happy, walk about the bailey. Musicians caper, rattling be-ribboned tambourines, blowing on fifes, or strumming lutes. Fools juggle, fire-blowers send up great gouts of orange flame, and hawkers call out from booths. All in all, it looks like quite a party.

A page boy runs up to Torvold and doffs his hat. "Are you on the lists, milord?" the boy squeaks.

"Not today," Torvold replies, looking a bit dejected, as if he wished he was. "Do you know where the road to Market Town lies?"

"There is no road but the one that led you here, milord," the boy replies. Torvold and I share a worried look.

I hear screams and catch sight of Rancor making his way to a beer garden. The patrons back away from him fearfully as he sticks his nose into someone's tankard. Great. My unicorn has a drinking problem.

"Well, he's not going to be any help to us if he keeps that up," I say, waving a hand in Rancor's direction. "Maybe someone else knows where the road is?" I suggest.

Torvold looks around, frowning.

"Can I stable your horse for you, then, milord?" the boy persists.

Torvold balks, looking from his great warhorse to the

small boy in front of him. "Thunder is no docile pony," he warns.

"Oh, I can handle him, milord, and make no mistake. A proud steed such as Thunder knows it's beneath him to harm a little fellow like me. He'll do as I ask so as not to hurt my feelings. Watch."

The boy holds out a hand, palm up to display a slice of apple. Thunder readily follows the boy and lips the treat into his mouth.

"Good enough then," Torvold says, laughing. He takes Calx down from the saddle and buckles it around his waist. "I am Sir Torvold. What's your name?" he asks, producing a coin for the young page.

"Rin, milord. I'll take good care of Thunder," he promises, his eyes shining at his generous pay.

Little sidebar here. I like the way Torvold does stuff. I like the way he talks to people. I like the way he listens. I like the way he treats people with respect, even a stable boy who's trying to make a buck off of him. It may not seem like a big deal, but I'm realizing as I'm watching Torvold with this kid that it is a big deal. If I ever have a boyfriend, I hope he's someone I admire, like I do Torvold.

Rin leads the enormous warhorse off, promising him sugar cubes.

"I don't know if my horse will want me back," Torvold says.

"You. Sugar cubes," I say, holding my hands like scales

and lifting them up and down in opposition. “I wouldn’t mind something to eat, myself.”

“There’s plenty here, and I suppose we should get provisions,” he says.

Torvold brings me to a stall to buy us some real breakfast. He pulls apart a steaming loaf of bread and hands me half. I see him bite into his share, as if not fully believing it won’t disappear. I bite into my half. It certainly tastes real, and the yawning sensation in my stomach is appeased. I move closer to Torvold as we walk on so we aren’t overheard.

“I know illusions can feel real, but have you ever encountered one of this magnitude?” I ask.

“Never,” Torvold replies immediately. He scans the crowd for a moment and then looks back at me. “Even the air smells like it’s real.”

I nod in response. I’ve never noticed scent in an illusion before. “But it can’t be real, can it? Do you think it’s a trick?”

He gives me a vague shrug. I look across the bailey at Rancor, who has scared everyone in the vicinity away and is helping himself to all the abandoned beer. I shake my head, wondering if he brought us here just to get his swerve on, and look back at Torvold. He’s still watching me.

“What?” I ask. “Should I go get him?”

“No. But as it appears we’re not going anywhere with our guide otherwise occupied, I would like to win you a prize," he says, taking my free hand in his and bringing me over to a booth.

"I would like to win *you* one," I say in reply, trying not to blush just because he took my hand. It's impossible, though. His hand is warm and firm.

"We'll trade prizes, then," he says, pleased by the thought. "But you'd better win me something good."

We start walking amongst the try-your-luck stalls, avidly debating which prize would be worthy of our exchange, when a fanfare of trumpets silences the crowd.

A crier in a motley livery stands forth and announces that the tournament is about to begin. Everyone makes their way across the bailey and through a portcullis opposite the main gate. We are swept along with the crowd and emerge in the bright light of a tourney field.

"I thought this castle was in the middle of a forest," I whisper to Torvold as we step out into the spacious field that is very much not a forest. The lawn is dotted with white pavilion tents that bear the pennants of various knights.

"Very odd," he agrees. "Do you still have your knives on you?"

I check for my hidden arsenal, and he watches as my hands wander from place to place, his amusement growing as the revealed number of blades increases.

"I could rival a pincushion," I assure him.

He laughs silently and shakes his head. "I am most grateful that I kept my chainmail on as we rode."

We climb into the tiered spectator stands alongside a long, straight strip of grass that has a painted fence running down the middle of it. Torvold tenses with excitement.

Jousting. They're going to joust. I've never been to a jousting tournament but I imagine it's akin to watching a car crash, only with more pointy bits. I hope I don't barf. Jousting is brutal, bloody, and I have absolutely no idea why the heck anyone thought it would be a good idea to do it for fun.

"Do you enjoy this sport, Sir Torvold?" I ask.

"I enjoy all kinds of sport," he replies. "Jousting is a particular favorite, though."

"*Why*?" I ask, unable to stop myself. It's his turn to blush.

"I don't know," he replies, repressing a shy smile. "I don't like seeing anyone get hurt, but in a good bout, no one should. It takes far more skill to win without bloodshed. I suppose that's what I like about it. The best jouster injures others the least."

I'm staring at him again. I have to stop staring, even if he is beautiful and thoughtful and full of interesting things to say, and even if he does feel "right" to me because obviously he isn't, and this is just some kind of sadistic test. If I ever see Mother Maybe again, I'm going to tell her exactly what I think about all this. And then I'm going to stab her in the eye.

The crowd parts for us as we approach the risers.

People stand aside and bow to us, making a path that leads to the preferential seats in the middle. Here there is a canvas tent above that provides shade, and a perfect view of where the combatants will inevitably come crashing together.

"Do they know who I am, or who you are?" I ask quietly.

He's acting nonchalant and accepting this preferential treatment with gracious nods of his head, but I can tell he's on edge. My hand is on his forearm, and I can feel all of his muscles bunching.

"I don't recognize any of these standards," he says, looking at the painted shields displayed on the railing of the jousting list.

It occurs to me, belatedly, that all of the knights in the land, apart from Torvold, have been either defeated by Asphodel and turned into bark, or they're on the run. Who, then, would be left to joust?

Also, another minor point that I can't help but notice is that all the women here are wearing a different type of dress from me. Not that I'm an expert in medieval clothing, but I have gotten very familiar with tightening a corset, and these ladies aren't wearing the same kind of hoist-and-suffocate situation I am. They're also wearing wimples, which are the type of head and neck covering that most people associate with nuns. I'm acutely conscious of my uncovered hair and the hint of cleavage from my much lower neckline all of a sudden.

"Their style of dress is old-fashioned, and they wear wimples. Nobody wears wimples anymore," I whisper to Torvold.

He nods, his hand gripping mine. "All of these standards are plain. See that one there is just a field of blue with a line across it? And that one over there is just a black and yellow checkerboard?" He gestures to the simply decorated shields propped up before each knight's tent in turn, pointing them out to me.

"Why is that of concern to you?" I ask.

"Standards usually get more complicated as they're handed down. Each generation tries to do something noteworthy enough to add to the basic family design."

"What does it mean that these are so rudimentary?"

"That these standards must be from ages ago," he answers reluctantly.

"And what does *that* mean?"

"I think it means we're in the past."

13
TIME OUT

There is no way we time traveled. This just isn't that kind of story.

Plus, if we did time travel, I think everyone would be reacting to us a little bit more. Here I am, walking around with my head, neck, and a small but still noticeable amount of my ample bosom uncovered when all of the other women here are swaddled like mummies, and no one is throwing vegetables at me and calling me a trollop. They aren't even staring. And I've got the kind of cleavage that some people stare at, even in modern-day Los Angeles. It's been something of an issue for me, to be honest.

This must still be an elaborate illusion, one that Torvold and I are somehow allowed to participate in without causing too much of a commotion. But why? I look around for my inebriated unicorn and see him gamboling about, apparently having a marvelous time scaring the bejeezus out of people. But he could do that anywhere. It doesn't explain why he brought us here.

The long trumpets and the motley crier from earlier make another appearance to announce the beginning of the first bout. Behind us, in the most prized position on the highest level of the covered dais, an older man wearing a crown on top of his silver-shot black hair, and an absolutely stunning young woman appear and take their seats. Pike-carrying guards take position behind and around them. There are a lot of guards, and their presence is not appreciated by the crowd. Everyone turns to the newcomers and bows. I follow a little late, surprised that I see so many phony smiles on what are supposed to be the adoring subjects' faces.

The man, who I'm guessing is the king, waves his hand dismissively at the bowing crowd. What a jerk. I would use stronger language to describe him but, like I said, I'm stuck in a family-friendly book. I glance at Torvold, and by the troubled look on his face, I gather that he agrees with my assessment of the king.

"Get on with it," the king orders, flinging his words to the crier as he sits.

The stunning woman who seems to be accustomed to ignoring the king's ungracious behavior takes the lesser seat next to him. As soon as they're seated, everyone turns back around. Torvold and I are close enough to the king's seat that we have to be careful how we speak so we aren't overheard, but for now, a look between us is all we need.

It's obvious this king is not very well-liked, and he knows it.

The opposing knights enter the lists astride their chargers. On one side there is a knight in spectacular dark green armor. It shimmers in the sunlight, the light bouncing off of it as if it were nearly iridescent. I've never seen armor like that before and can't help but wonder if it isn't magical. As he approaches, the emblem of a beautiful tree becomes visible on the front of the Green Knight's shield.

When the Green Knight approaches the spectator stands the crowd jumps up, hurrahing him. Those in the standing area closest to the barrier press up against the fence, calling out to their favorite.

On the other end of the lists, an enormous knight, twice the size of the Green Knight, comes galloping into view. His all-black armor does not shine. In fact, it seems to suck the light into it in a way that I would say was also magical, but the wrong kind of magic, you know? His shield is a black field with a white noose painted on it, and his warhorse doesn't seem entirely tame. The giant black beast paws the ground, bares its teeth, and rolls its eyes so that they flash white and red.

The crowd does not cheer the Black Knight, nor do they boo him. Their expressions seem caught between fear and hatred, but they contain their honest reaction for one reason. At the Black Knight's entrance, the king took to his feet and started applauding.

As Torvold and I applaud politely along with the subdued crowd, we hear the king speak to his female companion.

"You seem anxious, my lady. Have no fear. The Black Knight will triumph," he says.

"Your majesty seems certain of the outcome," the woman replies sedately.

"I *am* certain of it," the king snaps. Touchy. "That low-born bastard should never have entered the lists."

"The people love him, Your Majesty," the woman replies. "They look at him and see themselves as they wish they could be."

"He's a stable boy!" the king says, losing his temper. "My Black Knight will do away with him."

"And the people will hate you all the more for it."

The two combatants come before the king to tip their lances. Up close, the Black Knight is even more terrifying. He is not normal large, he's genetic tampering large, and his horse isn't cute-crazy like Rancor, but crazy like he's possibly suffering from a slight touch of demonic possession. Whatever it is, the Black Knight has a creepy kind of magic that I have not previously encountered in this world.

Next to me, I can feel Torvold straining, like every fiber of his being wants to dive over the rails and fight the Black Knight. His knuckles are white with the strain to hold himself in his seat. I put my hand over his to calm him down.

The Green Knight is surrounded by the shimmery, golden-hour-light kind of magic that fits more with Lucitopia's brand. He's very elegantly built and even smaller than Torvold, I think, though I'm guessing about that, because he's wearing enough armor to line a tank and he still looks pretty darn big. The gray-white warhorse under him has one of those flowy manes and a curved neck. Aesthetically, the Green Knight looks very brave and romantic, and quite frankly, like he's about to get his perky butt handed to him by the Black Knight.

The two combatants pay their respects to the king by tipping their lances, and they are about to turn away when the beautiful woman stands.

"Your lance," she says to the Green Knight.

He dutifully lowers his lance right between Torvold and me so that the point of it is within reach of the woman. She removes the crown of flowers woven around her head, and her veil drops away. Sheaths of shining hair tumble down to her waist with a burst of perfume. The crowd literally sighs at the sight and smell of her. She hangs the flower circlet on the point of the Green Knight's lance. He lifts his lance to let it slide down the shaft (this is just what's happening, so don't blame me if the description sounds spicy) and he does this little bow to her from the saddle.

"You honor me, Merrow," the Green Knight says from behind his helmet's visor.

First name basis. That's a big deal here. It means

they're either related or they're betrothed or something like that because people don't go walking around Lucitopia calling each other by their first names without a title. Like, I would never call Torvold just Torvold to his face. I call him Sir Torvold, or good sir knight. That's cosplay 101.

"For Avalon," Merrow says, giving the king some side-eye. The crowd sends up a raucous cheer.

The king is not pleased. Merrow returns to her seat next to him and puts her hands calmly in her lap.

"If he is your champion, is Avalon mine when he is defeated?" the king asks while the combatants gallop to opposite ends of the list.

"Avalon belongs to the Dagda, not me. Would you give the Dagda your kingdom if James defeats your Black Knight?" she asks in return, pointedly using his first name again. Her intimacy with Sir James really bothers the king, too.

The knights face each other, lances braced and warhorses twitching. With a wave of a white flag, they pound toward each other like a couple of maniacs. They both lower their lances, aiming for each other's hearts, but at the last moment, the Black Knight lowers his lance even more.

Torvold is the first on his feet as the horse beneath the Green Knight is dealt the blow and tumbles beneath his rider, sending the Green Knight sprawling.

"Your majesty!" Torvold shouts, his body half turned around to implore the king. The king only stares at him.

The Green Knight has been knocked senseless. He lies unmoving on the ground. The Black Knight dismounts, throws his shattered lance aside, and holds his hand out to his squire, gesturing impatiently.

"Your majesty, that was flagrant! You must intervene!" Torvold insists.

The king does not respond.

Torvold looks back at the Black Knight who now has his sword and is striding toward the dazed Green Knight. Instead of trying to go over the fence separating their two sides, the Black Knick begins kicking and hacking a hole through it. As he does so, the Green Knight struggles to regain consciousness and get to his feet.

"If you will do nothing, I will act for you," Torvold says. Then he pushes his way through the standing crowd before us, jumps over the railing, and runs out onto the field with Calx in his hand.

Torvold reaches the Black Knight before he can land a blow on the still unarmed and defenseless Green Knight. I'm on my feet, a scream caught in my throat as Torvold—who has no armor on, remember, he's just wearing a bit of chainmail that suddenly looks flimsy in comparison—while he and the Black Knight exchange blows.

I can hear the ringing of metal on metal, but it's hard to keep track of each stroke. I've never seen an actual sword fight before, and I had no idea they moved this fast with all that metal weighing them down. The clanging sounds are coming so rapidly it sounds like someone kicked a drum kit down a flight of steps. I feel like screaming, but I stop myself so I don't distract Torvold. One hit from the Black Knight and he'll be cut in two, but Torvold manages to push the Black Knight back.

The Green Knight's squire arrives with his sword, and though still dazed, he and Torvold take the Black Knight together and disarm him without bloodshed. Not content with having been beaten, the Black Knight charges them, even when it's clear that they are basically handing him his life.

Entirely over this situation, the Green Knight kicks the Black Knight so hard that his helmet goes flying and he falls down, apparently knocked out. Torvold and the Green Knight each grab one of the Black Knight's arms and drag him to the stands where they throw him down before the king.

"This knave has abused the code of chivalry," Torvold announces with open disgust. There is a long moment where the only sounds that can be heard are the panting of Torvold and his new buddy, the Green Knight.

The Green Knight has removed his helmet, and even though his face is beat up and his features are obscured by a wash of blood from a cut on his forehead, I can still tell he's about Torvold's and my age, maybe a little older. He's definitely no more than eighteen or nineteen.

And not that it's important, but if it weren't for all the

blood and the split lip, I would guess that he's a honey. He's got thick black hair and great cheekbones and he has that general hot guy face and head shape. I can't pin his ethnicity down, but that could be because he's been in what is essentially a medieval car wreck.

"And who are you?" the king demands, looking at Torvold.

"I am Sir Torvold the Bold," he replies.

"I've never heard of you." The king is eyeing Torvold as if he were trying to solve a riddle. Uh-oh. I stand and intervene.

"And I'm Princess Pleasant," I say, though no one asked. Torvold is far too honest to be able to handle this without revealing that we're probably from the future, and I don't know if these people are ready for that. "We come from a kingdom...er...out west." Confused looks get passed around, but the king seems pleased with this information.

"That explains it, then," he says heartily. "The rules of chivalry must be different in your land, Sir Torvold, for I saw no foul play."

Torvold chomps back a retort when I shoot him a look. The last thing we need is to anger this king and get ourselves thrown into a dungeon or something.

"In light of your well-intentioned, yet wholly unnecessary interference, this bout will be declared null and void," the king announces. He eyes me suspiciously. "There will be no winner today!" And with that unsatisfying announcement, the king leaves.

Merrow obviously wants to stay behind, but it's as if she's attached to the king by a very unpleasant string, and she is escorted off the high dais by the king's pike-carrying guards. The pike-carrying guards are also kind enough to come around and drag the Black Knight away as well. I make my way down to Torvold and his new buddy.

"My thanks, Sir Torvold," the Green Knight is saying.

"I am surprised to find your kingdom so at odds," Torvold replies. He's being polite, but I can tell he wants the gossip.

"That tends to happen when there is a usurper on the throne," the Green Knight replies. He sees me approaching and bows. "Your Highness," he says gallantly. How he manages to be gallant with a big gash across his forehead is impressive.

"Your wounds," I say. "They should be attended to."

"I'm more concerned about my horse," he says, turning.

We all turn to look, and then stiffen with fear. Rancor is circling the fallen warhorse, snapping at the air with his teeth like a lunatic.

"Excuse me, good sir knight, but I should tend to my unicorn," I say.

I flip my legs over the fence. Both knights step forward to catch me, looking shocked, but I don't really have time to be ladylike right now. There are too many innocent people milling around the fallen horse and around Rancor, and he looks especially erratic right now. I hurry to him.

"What are you doing?" I ask Rancor. He stops snapping at the air to look at me with his legs splayed and one ear coked the wrong way. Goofball. "Are you drunk?" I ask him. He sneezes. "Well, come on. It's not nice to stare. Have some respect for the d—"

I stop talking because the warhorse suddenly writhes on the ground, whinnying.

"Princess!" Torvold says, his arm going around my waist. He lifts me up from behind and pulls me away from the big gray's thrashing hooves. The very much *not* dead horse lunges to his feet, totally alive and all four legs unbroken, which seems highly unlikely.

Rancor perks up and starts trotting around, blowing raspberries through his lips, as if he's making fun of the dazed warhorse.

"I don't believe it!" the Green Knight says, jogging up to inspect his horse. He checks the grey over carefully, but there seems to be no lasting damage. "I thank you for restoring my horse," the knight says, bowing to Rancor and then to me in turn.

I have no idea what he's talking about, but I smile anyway in response. Rancor's response is to try to gore the Green Knight's squire who, awestruck by the unicorn's beauty, is dumb enough to get too close. Time to go.

"Okay," I say, stepping between Rancor and the innocent men around me. "Let's go find you some salt. Maybe they sell pretzels around here somewhere."

I nod at Torvold and he takes the hint.

"We have tarried here too long, Sir James," Torvold says to the Green Knight.

"Won't you stay, Sir Torvold?" the Green Knight replies solemnly. "We have need of knights like you in this kingdom."

I pop my eyes at Torvold, but he already knows that we can't stay. "I have a sworn duty to my land, and we must return. I'm sorry," he replies.

Sir James takes Torvold's refusal well. "I thank you for your aid. And yours, Princess," he says, bowing and smiling through all the blood still on his face. Yuck, but I smile back. "Taming a unicorn is quite a feat," he continues. "It takes a rare person to accomplish it."

Actually, all it takes is a bag of salt and a general respect for the unicorn's privacy, but I'm not going to argue with him. Especially not when Torvold is looking at me like he is now. Like I'm rare.

We take our leave of the Green Knight, retrieve Thunder from the stables, and ride through the main gate. Torvold suddenly pulls up on Thunder's reins and turns around. There is no castle behind us. Just trees.

"It *was* an illusion," he says. We share a worried look before continuing on.

I wonder what the heck all that was about.

Rancor trots ahead of us through the trees, tossing his pretty head like he didn't just lead us on what I suspect was nothing more than a convoluted beer run.

"He seems pleased with himself," Torvold comments from his place behind me on the saddle.

"I'm still trying to decide if we should still be following him," I say. "I'm starting to get the feeling he has no idea what he's doing." I feel a silent laugh escape Torvold. "What?" I ask.

"It's just that I can usually count on you to say exactly what I'm thinking, but in this case, I have to disagree."

I half turn so I can see his face. "If you have anything to say that will make sense of what we just experienced, please enlighten me."

He shifts me in front of him so I don't have to twist my neck. "Well, if that was the past, then it is good to know that this land has faced an evil usurper before and defeated him. Perhaps we can do so again."

"It heartened you to meet Sir James," I say, trying to draw him out because I can tell he has more he wants to say. This guy. He's one of the few people I wouldn't mind listening to for longer than he's willing to speak.

"It did. Sometimes I feel alone in this. Meeting Sir James, and seeing no one stand up for him when he was so flagrantly fouled, reminded me what *alone* really looks like. Yet, he perseveres." He swallows and pointedly does not meet my eyes.

"I would stand up for you."

"You already have." He laughs. "You took on three ogres with nothing more than a pocketknife—although I sincerely hope you never do that again. Bluffing about gold..."

"That was categorically stupid," I agree, laughing with him. "I solemnly swear to never take on three trolls again. Unless I absolutely have to, of course."

I watch him, which seems to be my new favorite hobby. Staring at Torvold. I'm such an idiot.

I turn back around and face the front. I just keep getting myself in deeper and deeper. I have to do something. Take charge of my life and stop the Battle at Knob Knoll from ever happening. I will not allow Torvold to die, even if I have to rewrite this entire book from the inside.

I feel Torvold stiffen behind me, and he kicks Thunder into a trot, following Rancor's swishing white tail. "Did you hear that?" he asks.

A moment later I hear Jackanet and Dex arguing with each other. "We found them!" I say, relieved.

We emerge from the trees to find everyone still in the middle of the road.

"Is everyone here?" Torvold asks, trotting around and counting heads. "Why didn't you make camp off the road?" he asks Jackanet, sounding annoyed.

Jackanet gives him an odd look. "Because you left just moments ago milord? We haven't had the chance yet?"

I glance over my shoulder at Torvold. He raises his eyebrows at me.

"The light is failing," I say. "We should make camp now."

We pull off the road and get a fire going. Torvold and I have tacitly agreed not to talk about our little excursion for any reason in particular. Maybe we don't want to upset anyone. Maybe we don't want to field a bunch of uncomfortable questions about having been alone with no chaperone for so long.

Nothing happened between us. Nothing will happen. We eat our supper in the growing darkness, trying not to look at each other too much, and then make sure our bedrolls are as far away from each other as is possible before settling down.

When I wake, Rancor is standing over me looking like he's expecting something.

"What?" I ask him. But I already know what he'd say if he could talk. He'd say, "Time to go."

I go to grab my pack and Rancor follows me. I get my bedroll in order and sort my stuff. I'm stalling, I know, and when I can't stall any longer, I shoulder my pack and go to Jackanet where he is readying Thunder. Jackanet jumps and covers his heart when he sees Rancor.

"May I have a look at that map?" I ask Jackanet.

"Of course," he says, eyes still on the unicorn. He digs into the saddle bag and pulls out a piece of parchment.

I find where we are on the map easily. There's a red X marking our spot. (It's an enchanted map.)

I look to the western edge where a large black castle

dominates an area that has been made extra mysterious by the artist's liberal use of *sfumato*. I fold up the map and hand it back to Jackanet.

"Thank you. Take care of yourself," I say. I have to look away. "And take care of *him*."

I turn to leave, but Jackanet catches my arm. "Hang on," he says. Rancor paws the ground and snaps his teeth. Jackanet wisely releases me and jerks back. "Come with us to Market Town," he suggests, though reluctantly. "I know you have a quest of your own, and I'm not stopping you, exactly."

"Then what are you doing?"

"I'm asking you to come with us. Market Town is only a day's ride away from—that place you were looking at on the map." He drops his eyes. "Please, Princess. You still have time."

I frown at him suspiciously. "How do you know how much time I've got?"

"Everyone knows." He sees my confusion and explains. "While you were in your tower, Asphodel made a decree that if you weren't his bride by Midsummer, he would gather his army at Knob Knoll, ride across the land, and burn everything."

I drop my face into my hand and rub my brow. Knob Knoll. Where many of the Virtues ...and Torvold ... die.

"When is Midsummer?" I ask, looking back up at Jackanet.

"Four days from now," he answers.

14
HOW LOW CAN YOU GO?

I end up riding with Torvold again. How does this keep happening? I should be leaving, not sharing his saddle.

But here I am, snuggled up against him. I should be riding in one of the carts. I should be walking. I should be anywhere but here, but as soon as he trotted past me this morning and reached his hand down, I climbed up in front of him without thinking.

Jackanet rides back to join us, and Rancor snaps at him. He's been in a bad mood all day. Maybe he's still hung over from yesterday. Jackanet moves his horse over to the other side, keeping Thunder in between himself and my cranky unicorn.

"Milord, Market Town is on the horizon," Jackanet reports. "We should be there before sundown."

"Thank you, good Squire," Torvold replies.

Jackanet looks me over, and he doesn't seem too happy. "Might I suggest something, princess?"

"Please do," I reply warily.

"It's just, what with Asphodel saying he's going to kill everyone if you don't marry him, there are a lot of people who think you should just, well, you know, *do* it so they can live." Torvold shoots him a look and Jackanet holds up a placating hand. "I'm only pointing out that it would be a good idea if she didn't announce the fact that she was the princess whilst in town in case some pitchfork-carrying mob gets it into their heads that they should drag her off to Asphodel."

"Oh," I say, surprised. Now I want to retract my former snarky thoughts about the White Witches and their wardrobe choices.

"Not that Sir Torvold the Bold couldn't protect you from a pitchfork-carrying mob," Jackanet interjects hastily.

"But it would be better for all if he didn't have to," I reply, nodding. I take off the circlet around my head. "Would you keep this for me, Sir Torvold?" I turn to hand it to him, and immediately know I've done something wrong.

Torvold is overwhelmed for a moment. "Your-your maiden's circlet," he stammers, blushing furiously.

Whoops. I think I just symbolically offered him my virginity.

I'm trying to work out a way to walk that back when he takes it and puts it under his chainmail. I see the outline of his hand tucking it into some fold of his clothing, right over his heart.

"I will guard it with my life," he vows.

Jackanet is doing that thing again where his eyebrows practically disappear into his hairline. He clears his throat and says, "If you would accompany me, princess, to the second cart. There are dresses inside it for you to choose from."

Torvold brings Thunder to a stop and dismounts. Then he takes my waist, lifts me out of the saddle, and places me gently on the ground between him and Thunder. He looks down at me. I lean against him because I'm getting a little weak in the knees. With my hand on his chest, I can feel my maiden's circlet under his clothes.

I know it's silly for both of us to get this worked up about a symbolic piece of head bling, but I can't help it. Symbolism can be pretty dang hot.

"Ah-hem."

Torvold and I jump apart.

I keep my eyes on my feet as I hurry to follow Jackanet. Rancor trots behind me. He nudges me with his nose. I stop to give him a rub behind the ears before I go into the cart.

Gertie is in there with Dex and Tudie. They're sitting on poofs and their heads are bent together in conspiracy. Dex shoves something out of sight and they all look at me like there's nothing going on. There's definitely something going on. Gertie glances up at my brow where my maiden circlet rested until just a few moments ago.

"Lose something, princess?" she asks. Dex and Tudie burst out laughing.

"If you must know," I say, raising my voice to talk over the hoots, "after discussing it, we decided it best that I go into town disguised, and so I gave it to Sir Torvold."

Dex laughs so hard she falls off her poof. Hang on. Dexterity is looking uncharacteristically clumsy all of a sudden.

"Have you all been drinking spirits?" I ask, shocked.

Tudie and Gertie laugh so hard they fall off their poofs. Already down there, Dex gurgles on the floor. I tap my foot and wait for them to have their laugh. I probably shouldn't have said *gave it to him*.

Gertie recovers first. She pulls out the bottle of whatever it is, takes a swig, grimaces, and says, "We mean no offense, Your Highness. In fact, it's been quite nice for us to watch you and your young man falling in love."

"He's not my young man, and we're not in love," I snap.

Gertie trains a bleary eye on me. "I know plenty of girls in the city who'll be overjoyed to hear it." She nudges Tudie. "Ten years ago, I'd have taken a swipe at him."

"Who wouldn't," Tudie chortles, grabbing the bottle. "He'll have girls lined up around the block!"

They all start laughing again. I go over to where the costumes are hanging and start going through them, but really, I'm just hiding my face because I'm not bawling or anything, but I am starting to cry. It's one of those cries that the more you try to not do it, the worse it gets.

"Oh, Princess. Wait," Dex says, getting up and coming over to me. She touches my arm, but I shrug her off.

"No, he should," I say, sniffling. "He should meet those girls and enjoy himself and be happy." I can hear Rancor kicking the side of the cart and whinnying.

They all stare at me.

"You're going to do it then," Tudie says sadly. "Jackanet told us about how you looked at the map to find the Ebon Spire."

I pause. The Ebon Spire? Is that really...I mean, that's the Dark Tower. What a *rip-off*.

"Are you really going to marry Asphodel?" Dex asks.

I nod and step back, refusing to let anyone touch my arm or try to comfort me.

"I can't let everyone die in the battle at Knob Knoll. I can't let him die." Even the thought of it makes me cry harder. I wipe the tears off my cheeks. They are really streaming now. Rancor starts ramming his horn into the side of the cart, and it's getting to the point where we can't ignore him anymore. "He wants the salt," I say. I go to the door, stick my tear-soaked hand outside, and let Rancor lick away. I roll my eyes. "Stupid unicorn."

"It's not the salt, it's your tears he wants. For a unicorn, the tears of a broken heart are —" Gertie stops herself. "Never mind. Listen carefully, child. Even if you go to Asphodel, he'll just kill you and say you never came. The battle at Knob Knoll is going to happen no matter what you do."

I sit down in a heap next to the threadbare silks, sequins, and low-cut bodices. "I know it's a trap. Everyone knows it's a trap." I shake my head. "But I can't sit by and do nothing. I've done that already, and it doesn't work."

They don't have anything to say. Because, really, there is nothing *to* say. In these types of stories, the men who wrote them always forgot that the princess wasn't a symbol. She was a person who could get up and walk all the way to the Ebon Spire and call the bad guy's bluff.

That's exactly what I must do within three days' time. Well, at least I now have a quest. It feels good to finally start making some choices about my future. Short though it may be.

"What should I wear?" I ask brightly.

Gertie narrows her eyes and shakes a finger at me. "You, my lady, should wear the pink dress." She gets up and finds it on the rack.

There are no sequins on this one, and it isn't as threadbare as the others, but it is decidedly the lowest cut, most tightly fitting bodice I have ever seen in Lucitopia.

"It doesn't leave much to the imagination," I say, balking.

"Torvold will imagine plenty when he sees you in this," Gertie promises.

"Pink is so pretty," Dex enthuses. "And it will look amazing with your auburn hair."

I laugh, unlacing the much higher neckline of my dark blue dress. "Pretty in pink," I say.

"Exactly!" all three ladies say at once, not getting it.

15

LIGHTS... CAMERA... KNIVES!

I step out of the carriage.

Every girl has that dream of walking down the stairs and making the jaws drop and the music stops. Her skin glows, and her hair is a shining mass of gorgeousness, and the dress—oh, honey. The *dress*. The dress is the icing on the cake, and who eats the cake, right?

I've had that dream of being that girl. Let's be honest, that's why most girls want a big wedding. They want that door to open and for everyone to fall over in awe.

Spoiler alert, it doesn't happen for me in the pink dress.

Sure, jaws drop. I get a whistle from a few of the minstrels, and then Torvold gallops over on Thunder and says, "That dress is entirely inappropriate."

He dismounts, grabs my arm, turns me around, and starts pushing me back up the steps of the cart.

"What?" I say, nearly choking on my indignation. "I will wear whatever I want, thank you very much!"

"A woman's person is her own, and she may display it as she sees fit, but I made an oath when you gave me your maiden's circlet, and since I would rather not have to kill half the men in Market Town defending your virtue, you will find something else to wear or you will stay inside the cart for the rest of the trip!" he growls at me. Then he shoves me inside and shuts the door.

I hear Rancor knicker outside, like he's laughing at me. I stand there staring at Tudie, Dex, and Gertie for a moment. To be honest, I'm relieved. While I firmly believe that any woman has the right to wear whatever she likes, I don't really like this dress. I'm not comfortable walking around worrying that one of my boobs is going to come flying out if I take too deep of a breath. Also, I like to be able to take deep breaths, which the pink dress does not allow me to do. Finally, I'd rather avoid senseless bloodshed if I can.

"I think it best we find something else," I state.

"Well, there's this green velvet one," Tudie suggests cheerfully. She holds it up, and it's perfect.

Simple, elegant, old-fashioned maybe, but well-cut and made of high-quality material.

I put it on and it fits, although in keeping with the style of the minstrels, it is a little snug around the bosom. I'm high and tight, but I'm not tumbling out of anything.

The delicately puffed cap sleeves drape over the outermost portion of my shoulders, leaving a lot of skin. But it's only neck, shoulder, and upper-chest skin, and not flagrant cleavage or side boob. The dress isn't perfect. I don't like that I don't have sleeves for my blades, and that the bodice is too tight for anything sharp. I'll have to get by with just two daggers in my garters. Luckily, this skirt is easy to pull up. I'm not going to spend too much time thinking about why.

I decide to put my hair halfway up. I make a small braid with a single golden strand woven through it and twist the braid around my head. I can't wear my maiden's circlet, but I'll wear something like it. I've grown quite used to it, and find that I feel half-dressed without it.

This time, when I step out of the carriage, I get the response I'm looking for. Not from the minstrels. They turn away bored. But I get the reaction I've always dreamed of from Torvold.

His frowning face lifts and catches the light. I see him draw in a breath that he holds as if it might be his last. He steps forward and offers me his hand. I place my fingertips on his and he draws them to his heart, pressing the backs of my fingers against the place where my maiden's circlet hides.

"You look beautiful, prin—," Torvold stops and laughs. "I almost called you by your title, which I must not do. What shall I call you while we are in Market Town?" he asks quietly.

I almost give him my real name because I want to hear

him say it, but I reconsider at the last moment. This dress is making me feel a little sassy.

"I think, Sir Torvold, that you would be too high above my station as a simple minstrel to call me anything but *girl*," I say tartly. Might as well get into the part.

I pull my hand from his and glide over to where Gertie, Tudie, and Dex are watching from the steps of the cart. Torvold marks me with a slit-eyed smile, his lips cocked to one side.

"*My* girl," he corrects, loudly enough for everyone to hear.

Thunder must have read the script, because at this exact moment, he rears up, wheels, trots past Torvold at just the right pace for his master to swing up into the saddle, turns again, and churns up an impressive amount of sod as he gallops to the front of the caravan. Basically, Torvold just did the Camelot equivalent of burning a donut in my driveway.

Rancor whickers at me like he's laughing again.

"Well, how am I supposed to best something like that if you won't help?" I ask him. "Did you see what Thunder did?"

Rancor nibbles one of my cap sleeves.

"Oh, now you're sorry." I rub his soft nose. "Come on. I'll find you some fresh tears to drink."

Rancor blows air out of his nose, but he doesn't sneeze like he normally would, which strikes me as odd. He sounds congested. I wonder if unicorns can catch colds.

. . .

We enter Market Town a good hour before sunset. I'm about ten steps in when I realize this is *my* market, the one I've been going to for the past ten or so months. Although now, before the Battle of Knob Knoll, it is a different place altogether.

The people are healthier and better fed. The produce is fresher. The illusions aren't there to cover up dereliction, but to add splendor to what is already scrubbed and tidy. The performers are genuinely merry, the hawkers are humorous rather than ominous, and even the foot and armpit smells are dialed way down. I hardly get a whiff of them at all in between the scent of candy apples and grilled sausage.

But the thing that makes the most difference is the children. Children are everywhere. There are babies, even. My feet slow as I wonder where they all went. Or, are going to go. Seeing this place so alive and full of normal people going about their day without the littlest hint of the hopelessness that awaits them breaks my heart. How could one evil sorcerer take so much in so little time?

Rancor gives me a shove from behind to keep me moving. Not that anyone trailing us is going to complain about him taking snaps at everyone who gets too close to him. He's such a jerk.

"I don't know if bringing the unicorn was wise," Dex says, looking at him warily.

"I don't bring Rancor anywhere," I reply, grimacing. "He goes where he pleases."

Up ahead of us, Torvold is getting a hero's welcome. Flowers are being thrown in front of him, people are cheering his name, and lots of young women have suddenly materialized out of the crowd to bat their eyes at him.

"Don't let it get to you, dearie," Tudie says. She links arms with me and pats the back of my hand. "Sir Torvold is not the kind to get his head turned."

As she's saying that, Torvold's head turns. He's looking down from Thunder at a buxom girl in a striped dress that would make the pink one I wore turn red with embarrassment. What was all that malarky he gave me about not wanting to kill anyone to defend my honor? That girl seems to be walking around, scantily clad, without anyone dueling to the death over her.

"I think I've been had," I say to Rancor. I look over my shoulder at Rancor and see that he's chewing on a candy apple. "Where did you get that?" I ask him. He finishes it and sniffs. Then he shakes his head. He still can't sneeze.

The town elders surround Sir Torvold as he dismounts.

"A feast!" one of the elders cries. "A feast tonight in honor of Sir Torvold the Bold!"

A cheer goes up. Before Torvold can be ushered away, he turns and looks over the crowd, as if searching. Lots of girls lift their chins hopefully, but he keeps looking until he finds me. He smiles as if sheepish about all the attention he's being given. I roll my eyes at his humblebrag, and his smile opens into a laugh as he goes with the elders.

The good news is that the minstrels have been hired to entertain at the feast. The bad news is I'm pretending to be a minstrel, so I have to perform.

Dex has done some moonlighting as a contortionist, and has a whole routine already worked out. Tudie has asked for a chance to address the crowd directly in order to give them a rousing speech about having courage in these uncertain times. I have no doubt her "Saint Crispin's Day" monologue will be a huge success.

"What can you do?" Gertie asks me with a squint.

"She's handy with knives," Jackanet says.

"Oh," Gertie coos eagerly. "Could you hit a bunch of targets? Maybe get one through an apple resting on someone's head?"

I look around, suddenly seized with panic. "On-on stage?" I stammer. "I thought I was supposed to be in hiding."

"No place better than in plain sight. We'll put a wig on you," Gertie replies, a little too happy about this. "'Ere! We've got a knife thrower!" she yells to Bashan.

Bashan looks me over. "All right then," he says. "Show me what you've got."

"I never said I—"

"Go on, then!" Jackanet says, giving me an encouraging nudge. Rancor paws the ground in warning, and Jackanet takes a step away from me. "She's a veritable terror with a blade," he continues, still eyeing the unicorn.

The whole troupe of minstrels is staring at me expectantly. I sigh and reach under my skirt.

"This is getting interesting," Vanil says, waggling his eyebrows.

I give him a look and throw my blade right from the sheath. It goes through his hat and sticks it into the wood of the cart behind him.

The minstrels share a look.

"You two can go on after Dex," Faith says with a nod. Faith, it seems, has become the stage manager in her short tenure with this troupe. Makes perfect sense.

"Hang on," Vanil says, feeling the top of his head. "My hat," he laments, as he pulls the knife out of it and sticks his finger through the hole. "What do you mean *we*?"

Faith shrugs. "She needs someone to throw her knives at, doesn't she? I think you could give her a good reason. The crowd will love it. Write some banter."

Vanil thinks over Faith's suggestion with a "not bad" look on his face.

"All right, but she's got to get me a new hat," he says, pointing a finger at me. Rancor paws the ground and throws his head in warning. "And that bloody unicorn can't come onstage."

I look at Rancor. "Do you think you could wait backstage with Faith? Just for the show?"

He nibbles on my sleeve. I take that as a yes.

Vanil and I barely have enough time to hammer out some banter for our knife act before the show starts.

The carts are pulled up in a line and backed against each other. The canvas tops are taken off first, then the metal bracers are unlatched. One long wall on each cart remains upright, but the other long wall and the two end walls hinge down to the ground, making a long, raised stage with ramps on either end and a background behind it. Curtains are strung up to hide the props and the performers, torches are lit, and in moments, the minstrels are ready to perform.

They each take an instrument and fan out in the audience. Though they are down a lute since the run-in with the bandits, even those without instruments do a fine bit of singing to gather the crowd.

I can't sing a note to save my life, so I follow Faith's example and start skipping up to people, taking them by the hand and pulling them to the open area in front of our carts. Rancor trots happily behind me. He still won't let anyone touch him, but everyone wants to. The adults he snaps at, but for the children he tosses his pretty head and plays coy.

The children scream and chase after him with sticky fingers. Rancor leads them to the front of the audience. When they sit, he licks all of the children who are either salty from crying or sweet with candy—so, all of them. The littlest ones squeal with delight.

"He's not as heinous as I thought he was," Torvold says in my ear.

He's standing right behind me. He's not touching me, but he's so close that I feel him in the halo around me.

"Yes, he is," I say. I turn my head to the side and glance up at Torvold. "Rancor is just tasting each child to decide which sauce to pair with them."

Torvold's head tips towards mine as he laughs. "And what does it say about you that you are so fond of him?"

I turn back to watch my devil spawn licking his future chew toys. "What does it say about you that you are so fond of me?" I ask in return.

I feel his hands encircling my bare arms. "That you are as rare, as magical, and as hard to impress as a unicorn," he whispers.

I feel Torvold's hands drop from my arms to my hips. He draws me back against him, his lips brushing against my temple. Rancor trots up to us, throwing his head angrily. He takes a snap at Torvold.

"All right, you silly thing, I'm coming," I say, breaking away from Torvold's hold.

I chase after Rancor, following him behind the minstrel carts. I don't look back at Torvold or I know I will run straight to him and do things to him that young ladies are not supposed to do in public.

16
UNICORN SNOT

Dexterity *kills* it with her contortionist's routine.

She gives the crowd the full Circe du Soleil, and considering the level of entertainment available to the people in this completely fictional but vaguely British middle-ages feudal-system type world, that means she blew their minds.

Not an easy act to follow.

I hear my cue, but I do *not* want to go out there.

Faith shoves me up the steps.

I recover my footing and mount the stage. Vanil gets right to the sexual harassment, and I do the tittering behind my hand baloney, just as we'd planned. While Vanil is going on about my "milky globes" (which is just nasty, but this crowd loves it) I happen to look out into the audience.

Torvold is not happy. Vanil stares very pointedly at my

cleavage. Torvold is crushing something in his hand. Vanil touches my arm. Torvold is on his feet and coming towards the stage. The audience is staring at him.

"I think we've heard about enough out of this man, haven't we, ladies?" I say broadly to the crowd. The ladies cheer. I turn away from the sight of Torvold rushing the stage like a bull and pull out a knife. "It's time for me to teach him some manners."

I throw my first knife, which pins Vanil to the scenery. I hear a few *oohs* from the crowd and turn back. Torvold has stopped, thankfully, but I can't leave him there to be embarrassed.

"Our Good Sir Torvold would never allow a lady to be so insulted, even in jest. He is as gallant as he is brave," I say, dropping my character for a moment and starting a round of applause for him. The crowd loves it and they cheer for Torvold as he returns to his seat with a bow and a blush.

"Now, what shall I do with this one?" I jerk my thumb back at Vanil. The crowd starts offering suggestions. Some of them are a little graphic, to be honest. Reel it in, folks. There are kids here. "Shall we see if I can cut an apple in half?" I ask, producing the apple.

The crowd doesn't quite get it until I place the apple on Vanil's head. Then they're into it.

I turn my back to the audience, preparing to throw my dagger at Vanil, who is making a big show of pleading for his life, when I see something in the darkness behind the carts coming toward us. Fast.

I hear it *thunk* against the back wall of the cart. Then I hear a scrabbling sound as something climbs. Vanil gives me a worried look.

I throw my blade at it as soon as whatever it is pokes its head over, and it tumbles back down behind the stage immediately, but not before I see that it's a Thrall. I whirl to face the audience and find Torvold's eyes.

"They're here!" I shout. "Everyone run!"

Torvold is up on his feet with his sword drawn. He looks, locates a target, and runs into the darkness even as people flee past him in the other direction. Rancor is making some kind of god-awful whinnying noise behind the stage.

I look down at the children sitting in the front row. None of them are with their parents.

"Rancor!" I call. I'm thinking I can put a few of them on his back and get them out of here.

I jump down and start gathering the children into a bunch. Before I can even get them all into a cluster, Rancor comes ripping through the curtains. A cloud of cinders and soot puffs up behind him.

I smell something like fishy garbage and turn in time to see a Thrall about to jump on top of me. I throw a blade at it and hit it right between the eyes. The Thrall absorbs the impact, but that barely slows it down.

The only thing I've seen kill a Thrall was Calx. But

Torvold is nowhere close. I throw my arms out wide to stop it from getting to the children when Rancor charges forward and impales it on his horn.

The Thrall bursts into flames and disintegrates into soot.

Apparently, unicorn horns are in the same "not of this world" category as Calx's sky metal, which is an enormous relief, considering I nearly died.

"We have to protect the children," I tell Rancor.

He tosses his head and starts trotting around us in a circle. The children are terrified, so I pull them together and get down on a knee.

"Do you see that cranky unicorn?" I ask them. They're too frozen with fear to answer. "Well, he's been looking for someone to fight all day. He's so excited that he's got all those nasty things to stick with his horn."

I get a few of them to perk up, and that's the best I can hope for, really. A team of Thralls are coming toward us.

I stand up and pull out a blade, even though I now know blades are more like speedbumps than weapons to these guys. The copper pan worked a bit better, as I remember. I need something more bludgeon-y and less slice-y. I stow my blade and pick up a plank of wood from the shattered scenery. I wield it like a bat. I didn't go out for softball in high school, but I remember playing T-ball at some point in my childhood. My dad is a huge baseball...

I'm going crazy. As soon as I think about going to a Dodgers game with my dad it's like I'm seeing him.

No. That can't be. The grey-green creature with slits on its neck and the oozing body that looks like it's turning into slime can't be my dad.

"Princess! Get down!" Torvold bellows as he slashes through two Thralls at once, turning them to ash.

The Thrall that looks like my dad makes a phlegmy orca sound and lunges for me. The children behind me scream and I homerun the Thrall with my plank of wood. He goes down for the count.

I look at him lying on the ground. This is impossible. My dad can't be in Lucitopia. He lives in Santa Monica.

Rancor rears up next to me about to slash the Thrall with his hooves, but I turn in front of him and wave my arms.

"No, Rancor, get back! That's my father!" I scream.

Rancor wheels his hooves at the last moment and throws his head in confusion as he lands next to my dad, but not on top of him. I hear the wails of the rest of the Thralls as Torvold makes short work of them with Calx. Ash from their burnt bodies is swirling and blowing in the breeze.

My dad writhes on the ground. He's in pain. I bend down.

Torvold runs to me "No, my princess! Don't touch him," he says as he catches my waist in the crook of his arm.

"Torvold, let me go! You don't understand—that's my father!" I scream.

Torvold wraps me up in his arms, holding me back even though I'm trying to throw myself down next to my dad to help him.

"The king has been turned," Torvold is saying desperately in my ear.

I'm fighting against Torvold, but he manages to spin me around to face him anyway. He's wrapped both arms around me and he looks at me like something in him hurts.

"We told you, princess," he says. "The king is a Thrall of Asphodel."

"No, you don't understand," I wail. "He's my *father*."

Torvold pulls me against him in a hug. "I know," he's whispering in my ear. "I know."

I'm sobbing. I'm past help. Because it isn't the king of Lucitopia on the ground. It's my real father. He's a crappy father, but he is the only one I've got, and somehow, I've dragged him into this.

"What have I done?" I cry into Torvold's shoulder. "He shouldn't be here. If I'd been braver. If I'd climbed down from my tower sooner—"

"No," Torvold says in my ear. "It's not your fault. Asphodel is to blame."

Rancor approaches my dad. I pull away from Torvold, scared that Rancor will gore him, but instead, Rancor sneezes.

A giant gob of glittery snot sprays my dad.

Torvold and I are too stunned to do anything for a moment. Dex, Jackanet, Tudie, and Gertie come running up while we stare down at my dad, who is covered in unicorn snot. The snot starts to glow.

"Is that normal?" I ask Rancor. He tosses his head.

Under the glowing mucus, my dad starts to lose his fishy aspect. His bones seem to stiffen under his skin and the slits in his neck seal up. After one more bright flash of boogers, my father looks like himself again. Except he's wearing a brocade doublet, tons of thick jeweled rings, and a big fat crown.

I step away from Torvold and kneel down next to him. I reach out my hand and touch his face gingerly.

"Father?" I say. He doesn't move. I look up at everyone. "What's wrong with him?"

Tudie and Gertie exchange a look.

"If a unicorn drinks the tears of a broken heart, he can heal any *physical* injury," Gertie says, shrugging.

"Your father's sickness isn't in his body anymore, dearie," Tudie explains kindly. "Asphodel still owns his soul. Without his soul, the king will not wake."

"How do I get his soul back?" I ask.

"When I face Asphodel at Knob Knoll and kill him, all of the Thralls will be freed," Torvold says. His eyes burn into mine. "I swear to you, princess, I will save your father."

I can't look at Torvold. I can't look at anyone. I drop my head over my father and cry for him, and for Torvold, and for all the stupid things I've done.

17
MORNING GLORY

The minstrels take my father into one of their carts and close it up to hide him from the returning crowds.

While it had been whispered for some time around Lucitopia that the king had become a Thrall, it had never been confirmed. Seeing the king in an enchanted sleep right after an attack by the Thrall could push some of the more trigger-happy folk into a riot.

Faith watches over my dad because I have to stay with Rancor. Silly unicorn is taking his guard duty a little too seriously and won't even let the parents come and take their kids home. I tell Rancor repeatedly that it's okay, and please, don't impale the panicking mom who is only trying to kiss and hug her child.

There's always one kid whose parents are late. If it was my dad who was supposed to pick me up, I was that kid.

I'd be sitting there with a teacher who wanted to go home, and my dad would drive up with his phone on speaker, still talking to whomever was more important to him than I was. He'd blame my mom, or his assistant, saying that they gave him the wrong time. I'd tell him it was the same time every day. Sometimes he'd say he was sorry, but usually, he'd change the subject.

My dad's a deadbeat and he'll never be a good father. But Princess Pleasant's father locked her in a *tower*. On the neglect-o-meter, my dad barely registers. Plus, he loves me, and I love him, so I guess I'll take my deadbeat of a father any day. If I'm lucky I'll get to take him home. If I haven't ruined his life along with mine, that is.

The last kid goes, but I stay there in the grass. The sun is setting. I must be crying again because Rancor comes over and licks my face. I hear Torvold approaching. I know it's him because of the soft clinking of Calx against his chainmail.

He drops a bag of apples in front of Rancor. Rancor waits for Torvold to walk away before approaching the bag, but then he digs in.

Torvold sits down next to me. I don't say anything for a while. When he opens his mouth to start talking, I interrupt him.

"Don't tell me I'm being uncharacteristically quiet," I say.

"I won't," he replies, smiling to himself because he probably was going to say that.

"Don't tell me I have nothing to fear."

"I won't," he says, like it's obvious we both have a lot to fear.

"And don't tell me you're going to fix everything."

He doesn't say anything for a moment. "I won't."

He puts an arm around me and I tip my head to the side until it rests on his shoulder.

At some point, I must have fallen asleep because I wake at dawn. I'm lying on my side with Torvold curled up behind me.

I have never awoken with a guy pressed up against me before and it's kind of freaking me out. Not that I don't like it. I do. Too much, actually. I try to edge away from Torvold without him noticing, so of course he startles awake. His hand goes to Calx.

"Are you all right, Princess?" he asks.

"Yes," I say, embarrassed. He looks amazing horizontal. "We must have fallen asleep."

He sits up and smiles. "I was going to carry you into the cart, but I...I was comfortable."

I narrow my eyes at him. "With me asleep on your arm?" I ask, not buying it.

"Quite comfortable," he insists.

"I'm sure."

"Oh, it's lovely. I'll do it to you tonight so you can see," he jokes, and then he suddenly isn't joking anymore.

He's actually grown quite serious. He touches his heart, where he's hidden my maiden's circlet. "Princess, I—"

I bolt to my feet. "We must part, Sir Torvold. It would be unseemly for anyone to find us like this," I say. Then I start charging toward the minstrel cart.

"Wait," Torvold says, getting up and chasing me. "I meant no offense by lying next to you!" He catches up to me and takes my arm to stop me. "I would never do anything to besmirch your name, and yet… I couldn't seem to bid you goodnight when I should have."

"Please, good Sir Knight," I say shrugging my arm from his grasp, but he continues.

"I find I am at war with myself. I have sworn to protect your virtue, when in truth, I may be the greatest danger to it." The look he gives me is pure longing. It's so frigging steamy I almost faint. I actually have to put a hand against his chest so I don't fall over. He smiles when I touch him, and his voice lowers to a whisper. "We are, as yet, unwed. That is why I must ask you—"

Holy jalapenos. Is he going to ask me to marry him?

"I think it would be best if I went to my father now," I say, stepping away abruptly. "Good morrow, Sir Torvold."

And I run away from him. Like a wuss.

I burst into the cart where my father is stretched out in his enchanted sleep and I see someone I was not expecting.

"What are *you* doing here?" I ask breathlessly.

"You look flushed," Mother Maybe replies. "Is the story swoony enough for you yet?"

Torvold enters the cart after me. "Princess, please allow me to finish," he's pleading. He stops when he sees Mother Maybe sitting next to Faith.

"Yes, do finish, Sir Torvold," Mother Maybe says pleasantly. "Or is this a private conversation?"

"Your Grace," Sir Torvold replies, bowing to Mother Maybe. "Your sister Faith said that you would make yourself known to me at your discretion."

I can't *even* stand it.

"You're a White Witch?" I ask Mother Maybe. "I didn't know Deception was a Virtue."

"Princess!" Sir Torvold gasps. "Forgive her, Your Grace. I've put her in an ill humor." He looks down, ashamed. "I have insulted her."

Mother Maybe smiles at Torvold like she wants to pinch his cheeks and cook him dinner. "I find that hard to believe." She waves a hand, dismissing it. "Your princess and I have had dealings before, and I'm afraid she hasn't fared well where I'm concerned."

Torvold looks startled as he glances over at me. I cross my arms, refusing to address it.

"I didn't come here for the princess," Mother Maybe continues. "I came here to aid you in the days to come. The Battle at Knob Knoll approaches. Faith and I shall be by your side."

Torvold kneels. "And I shall strive to be worthy of your aid."

Mother Maybe shoots me a look over Torvold's bent

head. We both know how this turns out for him. Unless there is no battle.

"Rise, Sir Torvold. The White Witches have chosen you as our champion. We will help you draw an army to your banner."

Torvold rises with an uncertain look on his face. "My quest was not to rally an army, but to find as many White Witches as I could."

"You have found all of us that are left," Faith replies.

The silence that follows is deafening.

"Then we must depart as soon as we can," Torvold says resolutely. He turns to me. "I take my leave, Princess, but I beg an audience with you at a later time to finish our conversation."

I tip my head down in reluctant assent. Again, he takes my hand and touches the tips of my fingers to the outline of my maiden's circlet over his heart before quitting the cart.

I plunk down next to my unconscious dad.

"What are you going to do, Princess?" Mother Maybe asks.

"Don't you worry," I tell her numbly. I can still smell Torvold in my hair, on my dress, on my skin. "It'll be heroic."

18

IF YOU'RE GOING TO HELL, GO IN STYLE

I leave the cart and go to find Gertie to ask a favor. It's kind of a big one.

She's busy haggling with the town elders about the minstrels' payment. The elders don't want to pay anything, considering the attack, but Gertie isn't having that. I step back when I realize that this is going to be a lengthy exchange. Maybe Bashan can grant me the favor. Jackanet finds me on my way to locate Bashan.

"May I have a word, Princess?" Jackanet asks.

I stop with a frown. Jackanet and I have never really seen eye to eye on things. "Depends on the word," I reply.

He smiles and nods. "You and I have been at cross purposes, haven't we?"

"I'm not exactly sure what your purpose is," I reply honestly.

"I suspect you are not entirely sure what *your* purpose is, either," he rebuts, smirking.

He's got me there, and he knows it. "What do you wish to say?" I ask bluntly.

"I wish to ask if you go now to the Ebon Spire."

I cross my arms. "Why do you want to know?"

"For I must find something to distract Torvold so that by the time he learns you have gone, it will be too late for him to chase after you."

Unbelievable. He's so eager for me to go to my doom. He doesn't even look sorry for me.

"What did I ever do to you?" I ask him. "Why do you hate me so much?"

He looks stunned. "Princess, I don't hate you," he says.

"But you are awfully eager for me to go to Asphodel."

"Not because I wish you dead."

"Then why?"

Jackanet throws his hat on the ground and kicks it. His frustration can't simply be from me misunderstanding him. It must be from everyone misunderstanding him, including Torvold.

"Because you are more suited to facing Asphodel than Torvold!" he yells, totally losing it. "Torvold is honorable, and Asphodel has not fought a clean fight in his life. He fights dirty! And that's why Asphodel will win if Torvold faces him! But *you* know how to fight dirty. You could kill Asphodel."

"No, I can't! I don't have a Puce Pinkerknuckle! I don't have Calx!" I yell back.

"You've got a bloody unicorn!" Jackanet hollers, throwing his hands around. "Did you see what that miserable animal did to the Thralls?"

I come to a full stop.

"Right," I say. Come to think of it, that crystal swirl in Rancor's horn looks an awful lot like the sparkly edge on Calx. "Do you think Rancor's horn will work on Asphodel?"

"I don't know, but if there's one thing I am sure of, it's that *you* will find a way. No matter what the situation is, whether it's with a unicorn, a copper pan, or a monster's unmentionables, it doesn't matter. You will do what you have to do to stay alive." Jackanet laughs sadly. "Rather than keep to the rules of chivalry and die a heroic death like Torvold would."

I look away and try to *not* picture Torvold dying. Again. It seems to be the only thing I can think of lately.

"I don't want that," I whisper.

"I know you don't." He smiles, considering something. "Maybe we haven't been at cross purposes after all."

Something in his voice has changed. I look Jackanet over carefully. He's sloppy. He pays no deference to anyone, and he doesn't really squire all that much, either. It hits me.

"You're a White Witch."

He straightens his shoulders and tips his chin up. Jackanet suddenly looks younger and cleaner, and I realize that underneath all that dirt his clothes could possibly have been white once.

"I am Loyalty, though Torvold doesn't know it," he says, his voice taking on a deeper timbre. "I chose him because he is all the Virtues in one, and if he lives, we *all* do. Please, Princess."

"Princess," I repeat. "Do you know what I really am?" I ask. "Do Tudie and Dex know, too?"

"We all know you're a hero," he replies, avoiding a direct answer. "And we believe you were sent here to save Torvold. Not the other way around."

I have to die so all Virtue can live? That's frigging fantastic. But even as I think it, I know it's not about me. I had already decided to go, even before Jackanet and I had this conversation because there's one thing I know about this stupid book.

Torvold can't die.

I roll my eyes. "Help me find Bashan," I tell Jackanet.

"Why?" he asks.

"Because I need him and his minstrels to watch over my dad and keep him hidden and moving around while I go to the blasted Ebon Spire and find some way to get wretched Asphodel to impale himself on Rancor's face," I say testily. "I'll figure it out when I get there."

Loyalty chuckles quietly. "There is one thing about this entire situation that I don't wonder about."

I give him some side-eye. He and I aren't square yet. "Pray, what could that be?"

"I don't wonder why Torvold loves you," he says.

Okay. I guess that makes us square, though I don't quite know what to do with that statement.

"What-what do you mean, he loves me?" I stammer.

"You could be a bit smarter, though," he says briskly. "When are you off?"

He had to ruin it. "I leave post haste."

"Right." He nods sharply. "Bashan's there." He points to Bashan over my shoulder, who is loading up trunks onto one of the carts. "You deal with him and I'll go tell Torvold that a village half a day's ride up the road is on fire. You let out as soon as Torvold rides, and you'll be at the Ebon Spire by nightfall. Even if Torvold were to gallop after you as soon as he got back to Market Town, he wouldn't get there in time."

I nod, take a breath, and march over to Bashan and make a deal with him to take care of my father in exchange for this hypothetical gold I keep spreading about. I don't even know if that chest is still in my tower, but there's little chance I'm going to live long enough to be proven a welcher. Bashan and I shake on it and right on cue, Torvold comes riding up on Thunder in a tizzy.

"I must depart, Princess. There are people who need my aid," he says, wheeling Thunder under him in a shower of hooves and sod. "I will return before daybreak tomorrow," he promises.

"Godspeed, good Sir Knight," I say, pushing my voice past the catch in my throat. "And have a care with yourself while I am not there to care for you."

He looks down at me while Thunder prances under him. He touches his heart, his eyes reaching into mine. Then he tears away.

I don't say goodbye to Tudie and Dex. I don't know why I don't. I never really said goodbye to my friends in L.A. either. I sort of crept out of town, too embarrassed that my family was such a mess that I had to leave.

I shoulder my pack and start walking. Rancor trots up behind me, which I expected since he follows me everywhere. He nudges my shoulder. I look at him. He nudges me again, but harder, like he's trying to knock me over.

"What is your problem?" I ask him.

Rancor trots in front of me. Then he lowers himself down on his front knees. It's not a natural or comfortable position for an equine. He lays his head down deferentially over one leg, and I realize he's inviting me to ride him.

I get a little emotional. First of all, because Rancor is stunningly beautiful when he isn't trying to bite, and second because I really need some help right now.

"Thank you," I whisper as I climb up onto his back.

I've ridden a few horses at this point. It's terribly uncomfortable and a lot of work, even with a saddle. But I am not uncomfortable astride Rancor. You'd think that the whole bareback thing would be absolutely intolerable, considering a woman's anatomy and a horse's backbone, but apparently riding a unicorn is nothing like riding a horse.

As soon as I am settled, and my hands are resting on either side of his neck, Rancor launches into an even run. I float on top of him effortlessly.

It's the smoothest ride into hell you could imagine.

19
TOLKEIN COULD SUE

Rancor and I gallop past bucolic fields and rolling hills, until we suddenly enter the *sfumato* zone.

It's hard to describe what it's like; apart from saying it's probably exactly like being in a place that has been liberally shaded with a charcoal pencil. The sky darkens as if I've entered a dense forest, but there are no trees overhead. I've seen my fair share of smog living in LA. I've also even seen what it's like when wildfires throw so much ash into the air it makes midday look like sunset, but there is no smoke or ash in the atmosphere here. It's just darker air.

Nothing grows here. The ground is covered in dead weeds that are noticeably absent of the usual insect life. Not even the wind stirs. Rancor and I seem to be the only things moving across this landscape. We crest a hill and gaze down into a bowl-shaped valley that stretches as far as the eye can see. In the center of the valley is a tall, black tower that jabs into the murky sky. I'm guessing this is the Ebon Spire. It's really big. Methinks *someone* is overcompensating.

There is no sneaking up on Asphodel. The valley surrounding the Ebon Spire is so wide in all directions that those inside the tower would only have to glance out a window, say, twice a day, to spot an intruder approaching from very far away. I guess my only option is to gallop up to the front gate on my gleaming white unicorn and hope they let me in.

I allow myself a moment of hysterical laughter as I picture wandering around the outside of the Ebon Spire calling, *Hello? Evil Sorcerer? Still want to marry me? Totally okay if you've changed your mind!*

But I know my laughter is just pent-up nerves, and it's either laugh or scream. I should have taken a moment to come up with a plan first, but I never do that. In fact, I think I spend more time wondering why I don't stop to plan than I do actually stopping and thinking of a plan.

As I get closer, I can't laugh because nothing is funny anymore. The ground becomes very uneven and Rancor has to slow to a walk.

What I think at first are rocks sticking up out of the dirt on closer inspection are revealed to be bits and pieces of armor. Bent swords and broken spears are strewn about, and among the rusting weapons and rotting leathers are bones. This is the sight of an enormous battle. One fought long ago. Either everyone died, and no one was left to bury the dead, or the living were too afraid to come back to get the bodies.

They were left here to rot. Which isn't just unsanitary, it's the ultimate scumbucket move. From the look of things, it seems to have happened so long ago I can't imagine Asphodel could be to blame. Unless he is crazy old. Which he could be. He *is* a sorcerer. Best just assume he did it. I can't imagine anyone moving into a high-value property like this and opting to keep the dead army in the yard.

This guy is really starting to tick me off. Mr. Abracadirtbag up there turned my dad into an undead Swamp Thing, he leaves fallen soldiers to rot rather than give them an honorable burial, *and* he's supposed to kill Torvold in two days. Unless I kill him first. Which I will do, dang it.

I'm working myself up into a decent-sized murderous rage when I see a cloud rise from the top of the Ebon Spire. As it nears, I think it's a flock of birds. The flock billows and flashes, and then tightens and heads right for me.

But it's not birds. It's bats.

I hate to buy into stereotypes, but bats are creepy. The squeaking, the shivering, the way they crawl around on their knuckles, all of it gives me the heebie-jeebies. If mammals were supposed to fly, more of us would do it, but it's just bats and one squirrel. (Who doesn't even really fly. It just glides.) All I'm saying is, evolution has spoken on the whole flying mammal thing. Bats are weird.

They swarm around us. Rancor tries to slash them with his horn but only manages to turn a few of them into puffs of smoke. They flap at me with their wings and I have to throw my arms up to protect my eyes. They land on Rancor and start to claw and bite.

It's been way too long since my last booster shot. I start tearing the nasty little things off us. Rancor rears up and accidentally throws me to the ground. I see bats crawling all over his flanks and jump up to get them off him.

As soon as I take a step toward Rancor, I feel something cold and hard wrap around my ankle, stopping me. That better not be what I think it is.

I look down. A skeleton grins up at me. In a fully instinctual *ick* response, I punt his skull with my free foot. It goes flying, but the rest of him hangs onto my ankle. More skeletons are rising from the sod between me and Rancor. The bats are all over Rancor now, and I can see blood streaking his white hide. They're pushing him farther and farther away from me.

"Rancor!" I shout to him over his frenzied whinnies. "Get out of here! Run back to Torvold!"

He fights more furiously, stabbing at both skeletons and bats alike. Puffs of ash and smoke blaze all around Rancor as he hits his stride, but even more skeletons rise from below and more bats join the swarm from above. I know which way this is going to go.

"There's nothing you can do for me! Asphodel won't

let you anywhere near him, but you can still help Sir Torvold. Rancor, you must go!"

Rancor resists for a few moments more, then finally gives in and runs back the way we came. As his white tail disappears over the crest of the bowl, the skeletons start to push me toward the huge iron gates of the Ebon Spire.

"I know the way," I snap, throwing their bony fingers off me. *So* nasty. I flap my hands around my head to keep them from touching me and hotfoot it toward the gate, so I don't step on one of them. They see me go, and the skeletons sink back into the ground.

I tilt my head back and look up at the impressive architecture. It's actually quite lovely, if you go for the black-on-black evil monolith with very few windows look.

"Asphodel! Let me in!" I yell, and my voice only wobbles a little.

The gate glows with a ghoulish green light and swings open by itself.

I'd be lying if I said I wasn't shaking all the way down to the ground at this point. Anger and adrenaline got me this far, but I'm running out of both. It just occurred to me that I could become one of those skeletons decorating the lawn, and I can't make my feet take another step.

I hear the echo of laughter, coming from deep inside the tower. Asphodel is mocking me.

I'm a teenager, I came here alone and sort of unarmed, and he's mocking me for being scared? What a jerk.

I stomp through the gates, under the giant arching

entryway, across a black marble audience chamber the size of a football field, right up to the onyx dais with the smoked quartz throne on top of it, look at the (okay, this throws me, but I'm furious so I roll with it) blazing hot *snack* on the throne and say,

"Does your offer of marriage still stand?"

20
IT'S SO ANNOYING WHEN THE BAD GUY IS A SMOKE SHOW

"Princess Pleasant," Asphodel says in a purring voice, "I can't tell you how pleased I am that you decided to accept my offer."

He stands and comes toward me. I shift my weight but then decide that I'm not going to give this guy any ground, and I plant my feet. He gets uncomfortably close to me, and I'm expecting him to stink—a hint of corpse, maybe, considering the whole necromancer vibe, but no. He's got a spicy, incense smell that's a little churchy, but thoroughly attractive.

Let me reiterate. Asphodel is gorgeous. He's like a puma, with black hair, tan skin and interestingly shaped hazel eyes. I know he's probably about a thousand years old, but he doesn't look older than mid-twenties at most. He's elegantly built, and although he's not much taller than me, I can tell from the way his doublet fits snugly across his chest and shoulders and tapers into a sharp V down to his hips, that he is fully shredded under there. I have no doubt this guy can swing a sword and I don't want him swinging it anywhere near Torvold.

Hang on a second. I know he's about mid-twenties and not a teenager anymore, but that black hair, those cheekbones. He looks really familiar.

"Sorry for the delay, but I was detained," I reply. "Tell me, have we met before?"

He lifts an eyebrow. My unintentional insult becomes clear to me. I force myself to hold his gaze. I'm shaking, and he knows it, but I've already decided that I am not going to back up and I am not going to look away. He gives me a slow, feline smile and glances down at my dress, which is torn and dirty after the encounter with the skeletons in his front yard.

"I see you must have encountered many difficulties, and I do so wish to hear about all of them, my betrothed." He spins away from me and walks down the dais as he speaks. "There's a room prepared for you. We'll dine together when you have had a chance to refresh yourself."

As soon as he leaves the audience chamber and disappears through an arched doorway behind the throne, my knees give out and I sink down into a chair.

It can't be him. There is no way Sir James is Asphodel. First of all, there's the name difference. Second, Sir James was a knight and Asphodel is very much a sorcerer. I shift in my seat, trying to piece it together. Maybe Asphodel is one of Sir James' descendants? Or maybe not even that. The Green Knight's face was covered in blood when I met him. It could be that this author just likes men with black hair who have interestingly shaped eyes and are of unidentifiable heritage. I mean, Torvold is sort of the same, though I would recognize him anywhere.

This seat is really uncomfortable. I realize that's because I'm sitting on smoked quartz. Which is what Asphodel's throne is made from. I'm sitting on his throne. I jump up, but no one is here to see my faux pas. Which is disturbing.

I come down off the dais. I go to the back wall, where Asphodel disappeared, and peek my head under the archway. I find green-glowing sconces barely lighting a long hallway. There's a suit walking towards me, and I don't mean a businessman.

A man's doublet and breeches—but just the doublet and breeches with no body in them—are walking down the hallway. He, and I'm just picking the most obvious pronoun here because I'm assuming that if one were gender fluid *and* bodiless, one would dress according to one's sexual identity.

Anyway, he "sees" me and beckons with a sleeve for me to follow him. He turns and starts walking back the way he came, so I follow. The sconces flare on as we pass and dim behind us as if conserving energy.

The hallway ends at the base of a stone staircase that spirals into uncertain space at improbable angles, like an M.C. Escher drawing. I can't see the top. I hike up my skirts and get to climbing. I'm ready for a grueling ascent up Mount Dirtbag, but instead, after what feels like only a floor or two, Ghost Suit breaks to the right and goes down another hallway, sconces flaring with green light as he passes.

I look down the way we came and wish I hadn't. The M.C. Escher effect is much more disturbing when you add in vertigo. I back away from the edge and reach for a wall.

"Note to self. Never look down," I mumble as I follow Ghost Suit.

We pass a lone window. It's just a slit in the wall, more suited for shooting arrows out than letting light in. I look out of it eagerly anyway, only to see that I am twenty stories high and surrounded by bats in the air and skeletons on the ground. "Or out. Don't look down or out. Got it."

Ghost Suit glances back at me. Not sure about that because he doesn't have a head, but I think I notice a tilting of the shape of his shoulders under the doublet as if he were glancing back.

"Oh, do keep going," I say. "I'm just admiring the splendor of my new abode."

Ghost Suit pauses momentarily as if noting my sarcasm, and then stiffly leads me to a dead end. There are no doors anywhere. Either Ghost Suit is going to kill me, or this is my room.

"I did hope for more furniture, " I say, gesturing to the bare stone surrounding me, "but I'm sure I'll make do." I grin at him winningly.

Ghost Suit pauses for a moment. I see his doublet swell as if he is taking a breath to answer me, but then he lets the breath out in defeat and turns back to the wall. He raises an empty sleeve and rests it on the stone wall.

The highly polished black stone moves and folds and turns into an arched entry above an ebony door. Ghost Suit pushes it open for me and bows, gesturing with one sweeping motion of an empty sleeve for me to enter my rooms.

The entire suite is made from white stone, not black. The ceiling is vaulted and there are two enormous windows on the far wall. One of them even has a window seat with lots of fluffy pillows and cushions. The sky outside is still dark, but I think I can make out a hint of sunset light coming in through the glass.

The four-poster bed is draped with airy white linen and covered with white and pale pink bedding. The thick rug on the floor is mostly off-white, dappled with washed-out red. I notice an artfully faded rose pattern. Across from the bed, there is a vanity covered in crystal bottles that are filled with perfumes and cosmetics. The drawer of the vanity is pulled open to reveal a stunning ruby neck-lace and matching ruby earrings. Next to the vanity is a changing screen. Draped over the side of the screen is a pink and red kirtle and a white silk smock to wear under it.

A grey dress comes out of the corner—just a dress, mind you. There's no curvy woman who's about two inches shorter than me inside the dress. Ghost Dress curtsies to me and then starts fluttering about, trying to shoo me into a small room off the main room, which turns out to be a decent-sized water closet. And, yes, there is running water in here, although I don't think it's a closet. Water flows down two opposite walls. One side is cold water, and the other side is hot.

On the cold side, there are two basins on stands with holes in the center of them. One is about sink height, and the other is about toilet height. Water flows into them constantly and goes down the respective drains.

On the hot side of the room, a large pool has been sunk into the floor. Since the water in it neither drops in level nor overflows while I'm watching it, I assume it must drain slowly from the bottom somewhere. There are rose petals strewn in the water, and the air is full of their perfume.

Ghost Dress starts unlacing my much-abused green dress, which would be hard to do with just sleeves. I guess she has invisible fingers. While I can't *hear* Ghost Dress giving me a lecture about what I've done to my dress, and how shocking it is for a young lady like myself to be riding unicorns up to the strongholds of evil sorcerers, I get the gist of the lecture anyway. Body language can be very communicative. Even if one doesn't have a body.

We both hear a clanking sound as the dress drops to the white marble floor, and I cringe. Those were the blades I managed to stow in the skirt. She turns abruptly away, busying herself with nothing as far as I can tell, and I take the hint, and fish the knives out while she pretends not to notice anything. Then she gathers up my dress and leaves. To burn it, probably.

I go to the edge of the pool and find steps. I walk down them into the most incredible bath I have ever taken in my entire life. It's been a year since I've had a hot bath that didn't require me to first chop the firewood, then haul bucket after bucket of water up a *tower* to then light a fire, heat the water, and finally take a hot bath. I'd given up on the concept completely about eight months ago and since then I've settled for standing in a single bucket of lukewarm water and splashing the worst of the gunk of Lucitopia off me.

Now, though, I submerge. I wash my hair. I rub out the knots in my neck and the soreness in my calves. I lean back with my head resting on the lip of the pool and listen to the sound of the water running down the walls. I want to live in this room for the rest of my life.

My eyes snap open. I'm sure that's exactly what Asphodel intended when he prepared this room for me. None of this is real. It's magic, and therefore just an illusion. I might be standing in a bucket of lukewarm water, pouring water over my head with a ladle, thinking I'm floating in a luxurious pool of hot, scented water for all I know.

I stand up and get out of the tub. I towel off, wrap myself in a bath sheet, and go to the vanity. I comb the tangles out of my wet hair, then smell the perfumes. They are all rose scents, but each of them has a different secondary note. One is candy, one is powder, one is spice. I spray myself with the spicy one because I already know what he likes.

I put on my makeup while my hair dries. When I stand, Ghost Dress is waiting with the white underdress across her sleeves. She pops it over my head and goes for the kirtle.

There's a difference between a dress and what I'm getting into now. A dress, even one with a corset like the kind I've been wearing, is not the complicated situation that this contraption is. A kirtle is laced up the front to squeeze your boobs and waist, but this kirtle also has one cuff that ties around the upper arm and another that ties around the forearm. The silk of the underdress (called a smock) puffs out between the ties on the arms, and everything has to be arranged just so, or you look like a couch with the stuffing coming out.

Then there's the skirt. There's enough fabric in mine to make a three-person tent. Wearing a skirt that sleeps three requires more balance than you'd think. So many places to hide knives.

Once we have the kirtle tied off right, it's time for the jewels. Rubies do look lovely with my coloring, and I have to admit, the overall effect of the dress, the makeup, the heady scent of the perfume, and the jewels makes me look and feel like the princess I wished so desperately to be when I saw that illustration of Princess Pleasant in this stupid book.

All of this for a dress. I look into the vanity mirror at Ghost Dress standing anxiously behind me. She seems to want to say something to me, but of course, she can't because she's just a dress. I flounce my skirt one last time, making sure none of my knives poke anything vital if I move around.

"I probably shouldn't keep him waiting any longer," I announce.

Ghost Dress turns and walks to the wall where the door should be. She raises her sleeve as if to touch the wall, but then she stops and faces me. I think she's trying to warn me.

"I know he's going to try to trick me," I say, smiling. "You probably came here with a plan and you wound up a dress. You and your counterpart out there, the Ghost Suit. You two are a couple, right?"

Ghost Dress' shoulders bounce as if she's laughing or shaking her head or maybe both. She throws up her sleeves as if to say *you guessed right.*

"Well, I don't have a plan. I don't know what I'm

doing, and I never have. But this," I gesture to the princess costume, "is not what I want anymore."

She shrugs at me as if to ask, *then, what do you want?*

A few days ago, I would have shouted that I wanted to get out of here, and I still do, but of all the things I've grown to want over the past few days, leaving Lucitopia has fallen way down on my list.

"I don't know," I admit.

21

GIRLS NEVER EAT ON DATES

I would describe the dinner table—the gold flatware, the linen napkins, and the crystal glasses.

I would tell you about the heavenly smell—the bowls heaped with lush fruits of every hue, whole fish with salt crusting their scales, and the steaming, saucy platters of meats and vegetables.

But you already know all of this is probably an illusion, and the only purpose a detailed description could serve would be to entice you to put this book down and go get a snack.

But I'll give you an idea. There are minced meat pies and roasted ducks, glazed with something sticky and sweet. There are creamed potatoes and spears of asparagus. There are loaves of crusty bread and bricks of hard cheeses.

And cake. Lots of cake, some frosted and dusted with powdered sugar, and some topped with whipped cream and cinnamon. There are puff pastries, cookies, and candied fruits.

Even from across the room, the food has enveloped my attention to the exclusion of all else. It isn't until I'm just a few steps away from the table that I notice I'm not alone.

Asphodel gets up and stands behind his seat at the head of the table. My stride hitches with surprise and I stop. He bows to me.

"Is something amiss, Princess?" Asphodel inquires.

"I didn't expect you to be here," I reply honestly. "I thought you would—"

"Make you wait?" he guesses, grinning. I nod, and he continues. "There was a time when I would have played a game like."

"Well, it's appreciated," I say, my face the picture of innocence.

He smiles, amused. "Please. Do sit."

Instead of putting me at the other end of the table, my setting is close to Asphodel's right. The table is lit with candelabras, and the soft glow warms a small sphere around our seats. Despite the cavernous room and the oversized furniture and the heavy rugs on the floor, the use of candlelight rather than those eerie green sconces makes our place at the table look intimate.

I take my seat and fold my hands in my lap.

"Whatever you wish to eat will appear on your plate, Princess," he tells me.

I look at my plate. Though I see the air over it shifting

and darkening, nothing appears. I laugh when my plate goes as blank as my mind. I don't know what I want. Indecision is sort of my thing right now. Plus, I'm rather turned off by the food porn, to tell you the truth. I don't want any of it, and I don't know why. It looks incredible, but I would no more eat the food on this table than I would eat the picture of a pie.

"Is something wrong?" Asphodel asks. "If there is a delicacy you'd rather have that isn't on the table—"

"No," I say, sitting back in my chair.

Asphodel's face is frozen. "Please, don't be shy, my betrothed. You must be famished after your travels."

"I'm quite content," I say, shrugging a shoulder. "If I am to eat, I want it to be real food. Illusion cannot nourish me."

It's like I ripped the rug out from under him. He leans back and considers me for a long time.

"You were warned?" he asks, narrowing his eyes at me.

"About what?" I ask in return. "That you are evil, and I shouldn't trust you?"

"I am no more evil than you are," he tells me in his purring voice. "And I, too, long for what is real. One could even say it has become my defining purpose."

I have no idea what he means by that. "Yet you live in an illusion," I say, gesturing to the cavernous hall around us.

"And you don't?" he asks.

He waves a hand and the food disappears. The table is

empty except for the candelabras and our place settings. Asphodel leans around his high-backed chair and snaps his fingers. Ghost Suit hurries forward out of the shadows.

"Bring us *real* food," Asphodel orders.

Ghost Suit leaves us, and Asphodel and I stare at each other. Ever since I got out of the tub, there's something that's been bothering me. I have to ask.

"Am I naked and dirty right now?" I blurt out.

I've managed to stump him. "I don't understand—"

"The bath. The dress. Are they real or am I sitting here naked and covered in filth?"

Asphodel the Evil Sorcerer chuckles. When he isn't mocking me, his laugh is infectious. "Your room and everything in it is real, although the view is not."

"Oh, good," I sigh.

He tips his head to the side, considering me. "You came down here, sat at the table, and have engaged in this discourse, knowing full well that there was a chance you did so while naked?"

"I figured you've seen worse things."

He shakes his head with a bemused smile on his face. "You surprise me, Princess."

I think of the knives I've got stowed in this boat of a dress. "May I continue to do so," I reply, smiling back.

Maybe he catches the edge of malice in my tone because I think I see his eyes flash, and whatever warmth had been in his smile vanishes.

"So, Princess. Tell me about your travels. From the

state of you when you arrived, I would say they were arduous."

"Indeed. I encountered ruffians," I say.

His eyes widen, playing his part. "And yet you made it here? Unmolested?"

"I had a champion."

Asphodel leans forward. "Do tell me his name, so I may reward him."

"I also encountered Thralls," I continue, ignoring his request. "Which reminds me, what do you plan on giving me as a wedding present?"

He frowns, not able to follow my train of thought. "Tell me what you desire, and I shall do my best to make it yours."

"I desire for you to release my father's soul, and the souls of all those you have enslaved."

He laughs in my face. It's not his nice laugh, but I was expecting as much.

"You have no need to make vassals of the dead," I counter cheerily. "For when we are wed the whole kingdom will be yours."

Asphodel leans an elbow on the table and props his chin on his fist as he looks at me, fascinated. "You're assuming what I want is to be king."

Hang on. "Has that not been your demand?"

"Well, yes, but it was meant to be an impossible one." He makes a pouty face, a really good-looking pouty face, but still one I want to punch. "Poor girl. You came here thinking you had something I wanted, but I don't want to rule this land. I want to destroy it."

I stare at him for a while. In books, every evil sorcerer wants to destroy the world, but when you get down to brass tacks, that makes no sense.

"Why?" I ask. I'm still trying to get my head around it. "Why would anyone want that? You *live* here, don't you?"

Asphodel stands. "My reasons are my own. And you, child, could scarcely understand them."

As he walks away, I call after him. "Then I may leave?"

He stops and turns. "Whatever gave you that idea?"

"You have no need of me," I say, standing, resisting the urge to beg. "May I go?"

"Oh, no," he says, amused. "Sir Torvold the Bold is the best knight I've encountered in a hundred years. I wouldn't dream of facing him without some kind of edge. My informant tells me he's quite taken with you. Imagine how distraught he'll be when he sees you by my side at Knob Knoll." He saunters out of the room and calls over his shoulder, "Enjoy your real food, Princess."

22
SUCKER PUNCH

I end up eating in the kitchen with Ghost Suit and Ghost Dress.

Their dinner, which they share with me, is a hearty vegetable stew, black bread smothered with a thick slab of butter, and a glass of milk. It's quite interesting to watch them eat. Food rises to the place where their faces would be and then disappears into what I'm assuming is their mouths. I would be fascinated if I weren't a hot mess right now.

While my hosts don't talk at all, they move around in a comfortable way, like two dance partners who know the steps to every song. Even the song that goes *we have a crying teenaged girl at our table. Let's feed her and tell her everything will be better in the morning.* It's a complicated song, but they're pros, apparently, because they don't miss a beat.

"I'm such an idiot," I say, blubbering into my stew. "You didn't see Torvold at the minstrel show, so you don't know, but even though Torvold knew it was an act, he practically killed Vanil when Vanil looked at my boobs. It's like Torvold can't keep a cool head where I'm concerned. And Asphodel is going to use that to kill him."

Ghost Dress nudges my forearm with her invisible fingers, guiding the forgotten spoon I'm holding to my lips. I take a sip of my stew. I have a few more sips because it's delicious, and then I remember another point.

"And he totally took the bait when that bandit—" I gasp and drop my spoon. Both Ghost Suit and Dress jump. "It was Gingivitis!" I proclaim, pointing a finger skyward, like I'm Sherlock cracking the case. "*He's* the informant who told Asphodel how irrational Torvold is about me!" I lean back in my chair. "If I ever see that guy again, I'm going to punch him right in his gangrenous stink hole."

Ghost Suit and Ghost Dress both pause and share what I'm assuming is a look. I go back to my dinner. I eat a few more bites before another wave of *how could I have been such an idiot* washes over me and I have to put down my spoon again.

"And here I thought that my coming here would save him, even though I know how this ends," I say, fresh tears stinging my eyes. "But, worse, it turns out I'm the thing that gets him killed. I should have read the beginning of the book. I would have found out that I'm in it!" I laugh-cry hysterically. "Is *irony* a frigging *virtue*?" I shovel some bread in my mouth. Damn, that's good. "I mean," I mumble incoherently as I shove more buttered bread in my mouth, "coo I ger mo stoopid?"

Ghost Dress stands and comes around the back of my chair to give me an invisible hug. I cry and chew and cry some more before I swallow and wipe my face.

"I was supposed to be the hero, and I'm crying all the time. I hate it when the girl cries all the time. What a terrible story." This strikes me as funny, so I have a laugh. My laugh falls into a sigh, and I'm finally past the worst of it. "Now that I've completely lost my readers, I think it's time for bed."

Ghost Suit leads while Ghost Dress walks beside me, carrying the glass of milk. We go down a flight of steps rather than up. At a random wall with no dead end, Ghost Suit stops and puts his hand against the stones. They slide over each other and fold back to reveal my ebony door. Ghost Suit opens it and lets me into my room. He bows to me in lieu of saying goodnight.

I stop and put a hand on his shoulder. "Thank you," I tell him. I look between him and Ghost Dress. "Do you two have kids?"

They shuffle and twist their sleeves, and tip toward each other and then away again. Ghost Suit must be shaking his head because his cravat is wiggling back and forth.

"Well, that's too bad. You would have been great

parents. You listen really well." I take the milk from Ghost Dress. "I can get myself undressed. I want to be alone right now."

It turns out, I couldn't get myself undressed. Not entirely.

I get the armbands off the voluminous sleeves of my smock, and I remove the overskirt leaving just the silk slip, but the bodice of the kirtle is pretty much padlocked to my ribcage. I drink my milk, clean the makeup off my face, and I must lie down at some point because I wake up in the middle of the night sprawled across my bed like I'd just flopped down there.

The door to my room is open.

I listen for any sound. I check the shadows for Ghost Dress or some other article of haunted clothing. When I'm satisfied that no one is going to jump out at me I feel for the dagger I put in my bodice before dinner, note that it's still there, and tiptoe out the door.

Maybe Ghost Suit and Ghost Dress are letting me go? While I worry for them, if I can get away from Asphodel he won't be able to use me against Torvold, and maybe Torvold can kill Asphodel and set them free. Or avenge their brutal deaths is more likely. Asphodel is definitely the vindictive type.

Just because the door is open doesn't mean I'm not still locked in a cage. I need breadcrumbs or some string. There's neither of those things, unless I want to start ripping up my sheets, and that would take too much time. Instead, I grab one of my cosmetics. The huge pot of bright red lipstick/blush should work.

I go out into the hallway and mark the stone to the right of my doorway with a red X. Then I paint an arrow on the stone in the direction I'm going. Every time I change direction, I'll put an arrow, so I can at least get back to my room.

I have a plan.

Down the hallway until there's a turn. Put an arrow. Run down the next hallway. Find a staircase. Put an arrow and go up. Run down that hallway. Go along a steeply curved hallway. Put an arrow just to be safe. See another flight of stairs. Go up them, put another arrow. Take the only hallway available. Leave another red arrow. Find a doorway. It has a big red X next to it. I'm back in my room. Thump head against door. Maybe I can climb out the windows in my room?

I go back inside. My room has changed. Instead of window seats on the far wall, there are French doors and a balcony. The doors are open. I can smell the blooming night jasmine coming in on a summer breeze. I go out on the balcony and see Asphodel standing there, looking out at the stars.

I'm not afraid. I don't feel any kind of threat from him, even though I'm only partially dressed and he's barefoot and bare-chested and only wearing a pair of breeches. I was right about his body. He isn't bulky, but what he's got is shredded. I go and stand next to him and look up.

"They're not real," he tells me. The stars are too big and too close. Galaxies swirl. The astrological ocean above us shimmers, bathing both of our upturned faces with opalescent light.

"I'm dreaming, aren't I?" I ask. I feel for my knife.

"We both are," he replies. "We're trapped in a dream." He looks at me, and his eyes are full of so much hurt and yearning that it makes my breath catch. "I want to wake up."

"I'll help you," I say. I pull out my knife and dive forward, aiming for his throat.

I'm fast. He's just a little bit faster. He lifts his left hand and deflects my blade. I graze the back of his hand, and though I've drawn blood, it's hardly fatal.

He pulls me close with one arm and catches my wrist with the other. He squeezes my captured hand, spreading the base of my thumb until he opens my palm and I drop my knife. It's not comfortable, but it doesn't hurt. He's not trying to hurt me. His eyes are wide with vulnerability, not anger. It's almost as if he's a real person and not a cookie-cutter evil sorcerer.

"You almost caught me," he whispers. "You remind me of someone." He gives a silent, bitter laugh. "But I don't know who she is."

Still holding me against him with one arm, he lets go of my hand, so he can reach up and stroke my cheek. For a dream, this feels pretty authentic. And, not going to lie (and why should I because it's just a dream and people do the craziest things in their dreams) but it feels really *good*.

"Did she try to kill you, too?" I ask.

"I don't remember." He looks sad. "You know I can't die this way, right?" he asks.

"Of course you can't," I say. I want to reach up and wrap my arms around his neck, so I do. I press myself against him, my hand wandering into his silky hair. "It's just a dream."

He inhales a shaky breath, then he lowers his head to kiss me.

I bolt up in bed, rubbing furiously at my lips and making *blech* noises.

"So gross!" I yell after I feel like I've wiped all of Asphodel's dream spit off me. I look around. It's dawn. I'm alone and lying on top of the covers.

I swing my legs over the side of the bed and notice I'm still wearing my shoes. I go to the vanity. The red cosmetics pot is there. It's full.

"Just a dream," I sigh deeply. But nothing pokes me in the ribs.

I feel inside the bodice of my dress for my knife. It's not there. I look for my other knives, hidden about the room. They're all gone. Did last night really happen or not? Did Asphodel kiss me?

I run to where the door should be and start hitting the white stone with my hands.

"Open this door, Asphodel!" I scream. "I said, open it, you little...," I struggle inarticulately here for a bit, "sneaky...dream...invading...*monster*!" Is that a succubus? No—what's the other one? "Incubus! You're an incubus!"

The rocks shift and fold, revealing the door which bursts open, knocking me back. Ghost Dress hurries into the room, her empty sleeves flapping wildly. She reaches to help me off the floor, but I stand up and charge right past her.

"Asphodel!" I yell as I storm down the hallway. I have no idea which way to go, but I don't care. "Where are you?!" I scream. Ghost Dress flaps her sleeves in front of me trying to get me to stop, but I keep barreling onward. I see doors up ahead.

"You show yourself, you coward!" I say, going to the first door I come to and pushing it open. "You conniving...!"

I've found him. Asphodel is standing at the back of the room, clad in black leather. A suit of black armor hangs on a rack next to him, and Ghost Suit stands behind him, just about to lay the chainmail over Asphodel's shoulders.

It's all black armor. Is he the Black Knight, then? No, the Black Knight was gigantic. Asphodel is tall but he's not as big and beefy as the Black Knight was. And anyway, that whole situation with Green and Black Knight happened hundreds of years ago. All of these illusions are making it hard for me to tell what's real anymore.

"Bloody hell," says a voice just off to my left on the entrance side of the room. It's Gingivitis. That dirty, rotten, squealer. I march over to him. "What are you doing, running around in your under..."

I sucker punch him before he can say another word. His head snaps back and he clutches his face with a yelp. Blood gushes from behind his hands.

"You knocked out my tooth!" he groans.

"I saved it from a slow death."

"You brazen doxy!"

That does it. I stride forward to hit him again, but I feel a leather glove wrap around my wrist.

"That's quite enough, Princess," Asphodel says as he hauls me back against him. I turn in his arms and push against his chest.

"Let go of me you...dream —" I'm still not sold on incubus. I blather for a moment and then blurt out, "*molester*!"

He releases me immediately. "What are you going on about?" he asks, eyes flashing.

"You forced yourself into my dream last night. You kissed me while I was dream-addled!" I accuse. Even though I kissed back, he did the shirtless hot guy thing. So, it's definitely his fault we kissed. "You took liberties!"

"I did nothing of the sort!" Asphodel yells back.

His chest is swelling with incensed breaths. I glare up

into his face. He's not accustomed to getting this angry, and it's tipped him off balance. He's searching for words that won't come. He spins away from me, but I follow close on his heels as he strides back to his armor.

"Then where are my knives?" I pester. "How did you know about them, unless you invaded my dream last night?"

"I've always known about them." He turns to face me, calm and cool again. "After your first encounter with my associate here," he waves a desultory hand at Gingivitis, "he made me well aware of your..." he glances down at my torso. "...hidden armory. I had your knives removed."

"But my dream," I insist.

"Was your own," he snaps, almost losing his cool again.

I rock back on my heels. Why did I have a sexy dream about Asphodel and not Torvold? I search his eyes for a lie, but he looks down to straighten his gloves.

"Now if you please, I must get dressed for battle," he says, dismissing me.

I'd forgotten. How could I have forgotten that? Today is the battle of Knob Knoll, and I haven't even come close to killing Asphodel. I don't think I could manage it now, unarmed, while he stands inches away from his gleaming broadsword.

I glance back at him and realize he saw me looking at his sword. For just a moment he looks hurt. Then his eyes narrow and his lips press together in a sneering smile.

"Even if you were strong enough to lift it, you'd never get to it before I would," he says, his voice low and dangerous. He's a puma again, and I'm something in the bunny-slash-deer category. But I'm a *proud* bunny-slash-deer.

"I prefer daggers anyway," I retort.

His eyes flash as he takes a breath, but I twirl away from him before he can say something pithier. I feel the ends of my ridiculously long hair flinging out and brushing against his chest as I do so. I march to the door. I marched in here and I am going to march out again, even though I don't really have a reason to march anymore. It's the principle of the thing.

Unfortunately, I have to pass Gingivitis on my way out. He's leering at my legs through the clingy silk slip that I realize a bit too late is just shy of see-through.

"You should get dressed, too, Princess," Gingivitis says lasciviously, quietly enough that Asphodel can't hear.

"Oh, you think I should get dressed?" I ask in a patronizing sing-song as I saunter flirtatiously toward him. Then I sucker punch him again.

While he howls on the floor I step over him and say, "Don't ever call me a doxy."

23
TOTAL HERO

I sit on a white canopy bed, the bed of every girl's dream, staring at a gorgeous red dress, the dress of every girl's dream, wondering how the hell I wound up in such a nightmare.

I have no time left. I've spent a year trapped in Lucitopia. A year doing the silliest things, like individually clipping every split end off every single hair on my head or digging through apothecary books looking for the medieval equivalent of a tampon. I threw knives at a wall for eight hours straight every day for five months. I made my own toothbrush. Those last two were good choices, actually, but there were so many moments of my life here in Lucitopia that I wasted, and now I'm out of time.

I stand, wearing just a light slip, and let Ghost Dress lace me into the heaps of silk and bone that are my skirts and kirtle. If Asphodel thinks his sword is heavy, he should try wearing this dress for twelve hours. Men always measure strength in brute force but make any one of them carry around a skirt like this while wearing a suffocating corset and I guarantee he'll faint before lunch.

I could try to fight him. I could make Asphodel drag me to the battle, but that would only strengthen his position. Torvold would lose his mind if he saw me kicking and screaming. The more distraught I am, the more distraught Torvold will be.

Rather than try the blunt-force approach, I'm selecting the wait-and-watch option. If I stay close to Asphodel, which is where he needs me in order to inflame Torvold, I just might find some way to kill Asphodel before he kills Torvold.

I hope. I don't know why I'm still hoping. I *know* how this ends. But still. I hope with all my heart.

Ghost Dress leads me outside the Ebon Spire to the open area between it and the iron gates. As soon as I pass through the arch, I freeze.

A sea of Thralls stands packed like kernels of corn on a cob in front of me. Asphodel sits atop his black warhorse. The evil sorcerer is gleaming darkly in his black armor. His helm rests on the pommel in front of him, leaving his head bare, so I can see his gorgeous face. Next to him is another mount with no rider. She is an elegant white mare who wishes she was as beautiful as Rancor, but no equine will ever be as lovely to me as that fancy jerk.

Asphodel waves a hand and the sea of rotting flesh

parts in front of me, making a corridor to my mount. There is no stench, no smell at all, and I don't know if that's real or if Asphodel has created some kind of illusion in order to be able to stand being among his creations. I take a deep breath and walk toward my horse, and as I do I see a familiar face appear among the Thralls. It's Gingivitis.

I don't know why it hurts me to see him as a Thrall, but it does. Not an hour ago, that blank-eyed fish-zombie was a person. I never knew his name. I never bothered to ask, but he was still a *person*. Granted, he was a loathsome person who leered at me, held a knife to a child's throat, and had probably done way worse things in his malodourous existence, but that doesn't matter. No soul deserves to be a Thrall. Not even the ones I don't like.

I walk through the sea of damnation that Asphodel created, my heart chilling with every tortured orca call that barks from their melting bodies. I mount my elegant white horse. She doesn't even *try* to bite me, which is just sad. I miss Rancor. When I'm settled, I look over at Asphodel.

"Did you like my gift?" he asks.

I pause, thinking carefully. "What gift is that? Seeing as how you've given me so many."

He smirks, detecting my bitterness. He cocks one finger at the crowd, beckoning. Thrall Gingivitis lurches forward and stands in front of me.

"*This* gift. He offered you insult, did he not?"

"Yes," I whisper, staring at him. His two front teeth are

gone. I guess I knocked out the second when I hit him on my way out the door.

"I punished him for you. Not the wedding present you asked for, but exemplary of my affection for you."

"Yes. I understand that now." I feel cold seeping into my heart.

"Shall we wed before or after the battle, my betrothed?" Asphodel asks in an offhand way while I stare at the tortured thing before me.

I hate Asphodel. I've never hated anything before. Not even Lucitopia. I think of dreaming about kissing him, and I want to throw up. I can't believe I thought he was anything other than evil. It's *right there* in his name—Asphodel the *Evil* Sorcerer. They don't give out names like that by accident, but I allowed myself to get reeled in by the pretty package, thinking that there had to be some buried hurt inside of him that could explain or even excuse his actions just because he's got interesting eyes and great abs. I am a giant fool. On the inside, Asphodel is as gruesome as his Thralls.

I look over at him, plastering a bright yet brittle smile on my face.

"I don't fancy myself old enough to be a widow, so let's set the date for after you confront Sir Torvold the Bold, shall we?" I bat my eyelashes at him in a mockery of flirtation.

He kicks his mount into movement. If he's smiling, it's not because he's thinking happy thoughts.

. . .

Remember those rolling hills Rancor and I rode past on our way to the Ebon Spire? Well, it turns out, one of them is Knob Knoll.

There's nothing remarkable about it. You can't tell the difference between Knob Knoll and the scores of other hills around it. I don't even see any knobs. Unless you count the giant one in black armor sitting on the horse next to me.

"You look amused, Princess," Asphodel comments. "May I ask why?"

I look out from the top of the hill, my bottom lip quivering with a smothered laugh, but I manage to hold my tongue. I've already learned that Asphodel leaves no slight unpunished.

"Ah. Here's your paramour now."

At first, I don't know what he's talking about. All I see is a smudge on the horizon. That smudge turns into an ant swarm, which becomes an army marching over the hills.

There are many banners. Some are checked, some striped, and some have the image of an animal like a chimera griff. Beneath each banner is a man riding a horse, and behind him march all the men who fight for that knight. I count over a dozen different banners with scores of men following them.

"All the good men left in the world," Asphodel says.

In the middle front rides a huge knight in golden

armor astride a white stallion. On either side of him ride five women, one girl, and one man all dressed in white. The banner above the knight's head is a golden angel on a white field.

"He's late," Asphodel mumbles. "Not as eager to win you back as I'd thought."

"You needn't keep speaking on my account, my betrothed," I say in honied tones. "If ever you grow tired of your own voice, rest assured, I stopped listening to you hours ago."

Asphodel laughs in spite of himself. "Maybe I will marry you after the battle, for I find you continually amusing. And I like to keep those I've conquered close. Speaking of which." He turns in his saddle and snaps.

Ghost Suit and Ghost Dress ride up on a pair of old dun-colored nags. Their defining clothes are slouched down in attitudes of defeat. Neither of their collars are turned in my direction, which means they can't look at me.

"Tell me, Princess. Have you ever heard of a cautionary tale?" Asphodel asks.

"I've read every kind of tale you can imagine," I reply tightly. "And you should know, that in nearly every story, the evil sorcerer dies."

He nods and looks out at the massing army and the bright crush of banners, armor, and shining young faces in every hue. At the forefront is Sir Torvold the Bold, flanked by Virtue.

"Let your heart flutter for Sir Torvold while it may, Princess," Asphodel says, sneering. "He won't look this good for much longer."

Asphodel is right about one thing. My heart is fluttering. It's Midsummer's Day and the air is warm, so like Asphodel, Torvold has his helm hooked to the pommel of his saddle rather than sweating underneath it before the battle has begun. His dark hair and tanned skin show up sharply against his golden armor. He is twice as broad and an entire head taller than any other man on the field, but he is no brute. His shoulders are enormous because he's carrying all of Lucitopia on top of them.

Now that they are closer, I can see the Virtues flanking him. Loyalty rides close, but a little behind and to the left with Fortitude and Dexterity. With them is the Great Griselda, minus her sparkly shawl. No idea which Virtue she is, but I should have guessed she was one of them.

In line with Torvold, and to his right, is Faith, Mother Maybe, and our mysterious hostess. I know who she is, and now that I can make out her face, I can't believe I didn't recognize her at first sight. She is Love.

Love rides closest to Torvold, just to his right. Next to her is Mother Maybe, but now that I see Faith on her other side, I know Mother Maybe's true name. Hope. Faith, Hope, and Love ride with Torvold.

"My heart doesn't flutter because Torvold looks good," I say quietly. "It flutters because he is good."

"He is the flower of all virtue," Asphodel says mockingly. Then in the silence that follows he truly hears his words and the truth in them shines through.

"He is the flower of all Virtue," Asphodel repeats slowly, and this time we both hear the capital letter on Virtue. "He is their Champion."

I shake my head. "No," I say, but Asphodel already knows he's figured it out.

"Thank you, Princess. They say Love never dies, though I've tried." Asphodel drops his head, shaking it while he smiles ruefully. "But I don't have to kill Love. I just have to kill Torvold, and Love will die."

"You're wrong," I say.

"Don't lie to me," Asphodel says. "I've searched for this for too long."

The two armies face off against each other over a flat bit of ground between the hills. On one side are the Thralls. On the other are humans. There are more Thralls than humans. Asphodel stays on top of Knob Knoll, but Torvold rides Thunder up to the front line.

Torvold dons his helmet. He draws Calx. I can't hear his battle cry, but I see Thunder rear up on his hind legs, and I hear the answering shout from his army. Then he charges.

Like a hero.

24
JUMP AND THE NET WILL APPEAR

Right from the start, it's clear which way this battle is going to go.

It's not just a question of numbers (Asphodel has more), it's that the touch of the Thralls is poisonous to normal people, and only Torvold can kill them with Calx.

The regular foot soldiers only have the power to hold back the Thralls temporarily. They can bludgeon them into immobility, as I did with my pan, but bludgeoning takes time. They bludgeon away, and it saves some of their lives, but it's not a way to win.

Torvold needs to be everywhere at once, and he nearly is. Great plumes of smoke and ash fly up and around him as he makes wide-sweeping motions with Calx. He scythes through the ranks of Thralls with as much economy of motion as can be, but no one could keep that up forever.

And Asphodel sits on his horse, waving a hand to conduct his gory orchestra, not even breaking a sweat.

"Aren't you going to fight?" I ask when I can no longer hold back the tightness in my chest.

"If Torvold manages to get through my army and challenge me, I will fight him." He leans over in his saddle and smiles at me. "Don't want to tire myself out beforehand, now do I?"

I glance down at his sword. I can't help it. I want to grab it and kill him right now. He sees my eyes drop down and laughs his cruel laugh.

"Still wondering if you could snatch up my sword before I can? Any time you want to find out, try it."

I look away. I need to find something I can use against him. I have to come up with a plan. You know...that thing I've never had? Yeah, one of those.

"You're not going to use magic?" I ask tightly.

"Why waste my energy creating an illusion?" he replies.

I look out at the battle, and I can see Torvold halfway through the sea of Thralls. Though he fights on, even from here it's obvious that his strength is flagging. I take a deep breath, trying not to scream or cry or do something really dumb like hurl myself at Asphodel's head. Then I see it.

There's a bright flash of white, thrashing hooves, and rainbow light refracting off a spiral horn of bone and crystal. Rancor comes charging up from behind Torvold, impaling Thralls and bucking like a bronco.

Whatever magical crystal is in his horn must be in his

hooves, too, for every time he kicks a Thrall it bursts into ash. Rancor twists out oddly and screams. It's very unnerving to hear an equine scream, and I *think* he's foaming at the mouth. He tears through Thralls like a kid through wrapping paper on Christmas.

Rancor has gone utterly bananas.

And it isn't pretty. It's like watching a beauty queen completely lose her marbles, tear out her hair extensions, and make one of those drama-tragedy-mask faces with mascara running down her face. It's not easy to watch, is all I'm saying.

Rancor runs out in front of Torvold and starts blazing a path for him, giving Torvold a much-needed break. Even if Torvold wanted to raise his sword at a Thrall, Rancor wouldn't let him. It's as if that insane unicorn had decided that every single one of the Thralls was his to kill.

The men hurrah Rancor, fanning the flames of Rancor's insane charge. Torvold is very good at killing Thralls. Rancor is exceptional. It's as if he were made for it. At one point it looks like Rancor just can't help himself anymore and he starts running over Thralls, galloping over them, and gleefully turning them into ash.

"That blasted unicorn," Asphodel says, grinding his teeth.

"He is a perfect menace," I say lovingly like that ball of murderous crazy was my special little man.

I just hope that Asphodel doesn't summon the bats since they seemed to be more effective at deterring Rancor than Thralls. But as Rancor mows down row after row of Thralls, and bats don't appear, I suspect that Asphodel can't call for them. I approached the Ebon Spire at sunset, when bats usually come out, and though it feels like the battle has gone on for hours, it is still mid-day here on Knob Knoll.

Asphodel kicks his mount forward. Torvold has made it through the Thralls with his bannerman, Jackanet the Loyal, holding his colors high.

Fortitude stands beside Loyalty. She strips off a white glove and throws it to the ground. Asphodel the Evil Sorcerer has been officially challenged by Torvold the Bold, Champion of Virtue, and he has no choice but to face him in single combat.

The Thralls stop fighting and pull back. The armies of men disengage as well. One of the Thralls limps forward and picks up the white glove thrown by Fortitude and carries it to Asphodel. Asphodel takes the glove and removes one of his own, finger by finger. Then he throws it to the ground.

The armies part. Rancor patrols the ground between them, snorting, but he does not attack. The two knights dismount, remove their helmets, unsheathe their swords, and walk to the cleared, flat ground atop Knob Knoll.

Asphodel is smiling.

This is exactly what he's been waiting for. For all my worry about Torvold tiring himself to the point of exhaustion, or flying into an unbalanced rage over me, the truth is that Asphodel might be a good enough fighter to beat him even without any tricks.

He did say that Torvold was the best knight he'd encountered in a hundred years, but I don't think you can know something like that without first being able to kill a hundred years' worth of darn good knights.

If Torvold fights, he will lose. If he loses, Lucitopia dies. Torvold can't fight. It goes against everything he is, but the only sure way to save Virtue is for him to turn around and walk away. I watch him mount Knob Knoll in his golden armor, the picture of heroism, and I realize that he's the one who should've hid in the tower.

Asphodel is waiting on one side of the clearing. Torvold positions himself across from his foe. I must stop this. I see Faith, Hope, and Love standing on a far hill, watching.

Jump. And the net will appear.

I jump off my horse. I run between the two knights. I hold up my scarlet-clad arms and shout,

"If we sacrifice the best of ourselves so that the rest may live, what's the point of living at all?"

Torvold stops, recognizing his own words. I turn to him.

"*You* are the best of us Torvold, not me," I say. "Asphodel doesn't want to be king, he wants to kill you, because if he kills you..."

And then I feel a hot, throbbing hole open in my

middle. I look down and see the tip of a broadsword sticking out of my belly button.

How'd that get there?

I should have come up with a plan.

That whole notion of jumping and the net appearing? Utter garbage. Just a bad idea all around.

Of all the ways I could have died protecting Torvold, I can think of about a dozen that would have been more effective than this. Jumping in front of Asphodel's killing blow, for instance, or pulling a Rancor and going berserk on Asphodel would have been much more useful ways to get myself impaled. But this is just embarrassing.

"I'm so sorry," I say to Torvold.

I see his face crumble. Then Asphodel pulls the blade back out—way more painful than going in, by the way—and I topple to the side. Asphodel steps over me to strike at Torvold, and Torvold parries.

Then a sound comes out of Torvold. It's not really a battle cry, it's much more personal and painful to listen to. A storm unleashes on Asphodel. Torvold is hitting Asphodel so hard that I hear the clanging of their swords through the *ground*. The blows are fast and punishing, and I have no idea if this is great swordsmanship or not, but I don't see how anything could handle being pounded on that way for very long.

I feel something soft and hairy nibbling on my head.

Then Rancor's warm tongue slops across my face. He's trying to drink my tears. The only problem is, I'm not crying. I'm in a universe of pain, but I'm not heartbroken. I'm too cheesed off by the idiotic way I've thrown away my one shot at a heroic death to cry over the fact that I'm dying.

Torvold strikes Asphodel so hard on the breastplate that his black armor comes off on one shoulder. The loose armor disrupts Asphodel's ability to swing and he has to back up and unhook the straps on the other shoulder, abandoning the chest and back plate altogether. Without the armor, Asphodel is more exposed, but he is also faster and lighter.

Oh no. Asphodel just disarmed Torvold. Calx comes flying in my direction and nearly kills me a second time. Asphodel brings his sword down on Torvold, but Torvold grabs his wrist with both hands and then pulls Asphodel into his knee.

Asphodel lets out a giant *oof* sound and then Torvold opens up on him. He knees Asphodel in the gut over and over, every time jamming his knee harder into Asphodel's solar plexus. Finally, Asphodel drops his sword, and then it becomes a fistfight.

Calx is just a foot away from me. This sucks worse than any period cramp I have ever had in my entire life, but I roll over onto my hands and knees. When I don't black out from the pain, I do a little baby crawl to Calx.

I know if I touch Calx it will burn, but maybe the

burning will distract me from the giant hole in my colon.

The brawl has come to the ground. Torvold is doing something to Asphodel's arm that looks like an MMA move. Not that I'm an expert in mixed martial arts or anything. And I'm pretty sure they didn't have jujitsu in these types of stories, but I guess if it works it works.

I reach out and grab Calx, thinking I'll just get it over with, but when I touch the metal, it doesn't burn at all. In fact, as soon as my hand is all the way around the hilt, I feel a jolt of energy, and the pain from my wound isn't that bad anymore.

I stand up. I walk over to the struggling knights. Asphodel has gotten on top Torvold. Calx pulls me forward until I am holding the blade to Asphodel's chest.

Both knights look up at me and freeze.

"Impossible," Asphodel says through swollen lips and broken teeth. "No one from this world can wield that sword!"

"Good thing I'm from Fresno," I say.

Asphodel makes a move to dive for his sword, and I stab him right through the heart.

And that's all I got.

I see the ground rushing up and then it stops and I'm lying next to Asphodel. His left hand, bare from throwing down his glove to accept Torvold's challenge, is right in front of my face. Across the back of it is the cut I gave him in my dream. Huh. He *was* there, in my dream. Maybe it wasn't even a dream?

That lying sack of—

"Princess!" Torvold sobs, lifting me into his arms.

He holds me to him and cries. At least I'm not the one crying this time. I'd love to wipe his tears away, but Rancor's gone and shoved his fat head in between us and I can't even see Torvold. I can't see anything, actually. I'm definitely dying. Maybe I'm already dead. My vision fades to black, just like in a movie.

Ew.

I feel gooey.

I open my eyes and see Torvold's expectant face. I see all their faces hovering over me—Dex, Tudie, and Jackanet; Thunder and Rancor; Faith, Hope, and Love. Even Griselda is here. Still don't know who she really is, but I'm just happy to be able to see anybody right now. I feel inside the hole in my dress and am delighted to find that there is no hole in my belly anymore.

I sit up and laugh. Torvold laughs and hugs me. Somewhere in there, he took off his breastplate and I can feel his chest against mine. I'm laughing and crying and Rancor is sneaking a lick even though these are definitely tears of joy and not heartbreak.

I pull back and look around. All the Thralls are gone. A middle-aged man and woman are standing behind the Virtues, smiling at me. She's wearing a grey dress. I smile back and wave at them.

"That's it?" I ask Hope. "It's over?"

but it's thick, shiny, and nearly to my waist. A year without hot tools and it's like I've got a new head of hair. Two: my complexion is crystal clear. No sugar or preservatives has given me super-model skin. I'll miss candy and Doritos, but I already know I can live without them. Three: I can still throw a blade. I went down to the hospital cafeteria, boosted a knife, waited until a hallway was clear and I sunk that bugger right into the hole of the A in the "Must Wash Hands" sign. That is not the sort of thing I could have learned in a few hours.

And last: My heart is breaking. I don't know when, or if, I'll ever see Torvold again. I know he's a real boy from this world or I would still be in Lucitopia. The one condition of my leaving was that I had to get a *real* boy to kiss me so Torvold must in fact be real, and not from the world of the book.

He knows I'm from Fresno, but apart from that he knows nothing about me, and Fresno is huge. Over half a million people live there. How is he going to find me in all that, even if he *is* back in this world? I have no idea what his condition for leaving Lucitopia was, but it probably wasn't the same as mine. A year in there was one day out here. Who knows how long he'll spend in there, and when he does get out, I could be ancient history to him.

I'm going to have to leave L.A. and go home tonight, so I can shower and make it to school. Mom said I don't have to go to school tomorrow, but I really want to. I want to try to make friends. I've spent too much time locked in a tower.

"Here's the doctor," my mom says, relieved. She stands to greet him.

My father's surgeon looks suspiciously like Bashan. I stand and narrow my eyes at him as if to ask, *do you know me?* He ignores my look and gives a quick run-down of my dad's health.

"We put in two stents, and the surgery went well," Bashan-as-a-surgeon says. "He'll still be groggy, but you can go in and see him now if you want."

"Thank you, Doctor," my mom says, and we both go into the recovery room.

My dad is hooked up to a dozen machines. He looks papery and hollow. Vanil and Gertie are there as nurses. They had promised to look after my dad for me, and they have. I thank them as they adjust the curtains around my dad's recovery bed, but they don't seem to recognize me either.

And that brings up another horrendous possibility. I could run into Torvold, like I am currently running into some of the other cast members from my ultimate cosplay in Lucitopia, and he might not know me.

"There are my girls," my dad says, still goofy from the drugs. My mom frowns, but she doesn't correct him. We sit on either side of him and take his hands.

"I missed you so much," he tells me. "I had the

strangest dream. You were in a tower. You were painting red arrows on the walls with lipstick."

I smile at my dad. "I missed you too, Dad," I say.

"We should spend more time together," he says, his eyes shutting.

My mom and I share a look. She raises an eyebrow as if to ask me if that's what I want. I nod.

"We will," I promise.

My mom has to stay at the hospital to fill out paperwork, and since I have my car with me from driving myself down to L.A. to have lunch with my dad, I have to drive myself home. It's four hours back to Fresno from Beverly Hills, even at 3 a.m. with no traffic, but I'm grateful for the long, solo drive. I need time to think. I'm also glad I didn't come back with my mom because when I get home there's a white horse standing in my front yard.

Rancor, minus the sparkly horn, is waiting impatiently for me. He's already eaten all my mom's roses and he's pulled up half the grass in the yard. What a jerk. I couldn't love any animal more. He sees me and whickers.

"You miss me?" I ask as I rub his soft nose. He lets me put my arms around his neck and rest there for a little while. "Want some salt?"

Rancor sneezes.

"Come on. I'll get you some salt."

He follows me into the house. I don't even try to get him to stay outside because I know he won't. He stands in my kitchen as I shake some salt on my palm and let him lick it. I do a quick Internet search for a local barn where I can stable him.

There are a ton of stables around Fresno, and lucky for me horse people wake up early. I find a stable that specializes in "difficult or abused" animals, and they even do pick-ups. I give them a call and they promise to be over in half an hour.

"Want some candy?" I ask Rancor. He tosses his head. I go get my mom's gummy bear stash out of the cabinet over the refrigerator. "I'm going to shower for school while you eat these," I tell him. "Don't chew on anything else."

I take the most amazing shower of my life, except that Rancor comes into the bathroom while I'm in there and drinks a tub full of water. I condition my luxurious hair, but I don't blow-dry it.

When the horse people come with their trailer, I walk out of the house with Rancor following me. They give both of us strange looks, but I just smile like nothing weird is going on and lead Rancor to the back of the trailer.

He balks.

"You've got to get in there," I tell him. He stamps a foot. "No, I'm serious. You can't live in my room. My mom will freak out. But I'll come visit you every day after school."

Rancor nibbles on my sleeve and gets into the trailer. I go to the driver. "Don't try to touch him," I warn her while I sign some papers. "Just open the trailer doors and

"Okay," I say warily. What could he possibly have of mine?

For the rest of the day, I find I have a lot of people who are interested in talking to me. It appears Jake Lopez is kind of a big deal in our little pocket of this world. He's almost as famous and beloved here as Torvold the Bold was in Lucitopia. He's the captain of pretty much everything athletic and academic, and though heavily chased by every girl in the school, from what I gather our familiarity in the hallways was heretofore unheard of. Jake Lopez, it seems, has been saving himself for the right girl.

He is the flower of Virtue.

By the time the day is over and I make it out to the senior parking lot, I'm spinning. Seeing him leaning against a silver motorcycle does nothing but add to my dizziness.

"Oh good," he says, grinning as I walk toward him. "You made it through the metal detectors. I thought I'd be waiting forever while security kept finding knives hidden in your clothes."

I jokingly frisk myself as I walk toward him. "You can only really hide daggers in either a corset or garters. Jeans and a blouse just don't have the structure to pull it off." I'm standing next to him now and I really want to be closer. I gesture to his bike. "Is this Thunder?"

He smiles and shakes his head. A bit sad. "No. Nothing can ever replace him."

"I know," I say quietly. We stand there forever, just

looking at each other. A million questions, but all I can do is stare.

He holds out his helmet. “Put this on.”

I put on his helmet as he straddles the bike. “What about you? Do you have another helmet?” I ask.

“I’ve done more dangerous things without armor,” he replies without sounding like he’s boasting. “And we’re not going far.”

I climb on behind him. I can’t see a thing back here. Jake is just too big. “I think I prefer riding in front of you,” I say. Then I wrap my arms and legs around him and give what I just said a second thought.

He brushes his hands along the outside of my thighs and turns his head to the side toward me. “I’ll take either,” he says, a little breathless, and then he puts both hands on the handles, flips a foot, and we’re off.

Jake brings me back to his house. It’s a modest suburban home with a two-car garage and a pool out back. Inside, the walls are covered with pictures of Jake and his family.

There’s one wall with framed ribbons and American flags. Lots of medals from war, and then pictures of a particular brand of firemen out here in the West called the Smokejumpers. They literally jump into raging fires to save lives.

“I was wrong,” I admit. “I guess there are a lot of heroes in Fresno.”

"I'm looking at one," Jake says. He's looking at me.

I blush and go back to the pictures. A guy named Manuel Lopez is in a lot of them. I'm assuming that's Jake's dad because he looks like Jake did after fighting the Thralls. In one picture, Manuel is covered in ash and smiling with an arm thrown over a buddy. The buddy's birth and death date are stamped in gold under the picture. A lot of Smokejumpers die.

"Is this your dad?" I ask, pointing to Manuel.

Jake nods, smiling. "He's sleeping right now," he says quietly. "He had a three-day shift."

I squint at the picture. "You are so much taller than him," I say, keeping my voice down.

Jake laughs under his breath. "My mom."

He brings me to a picture of his parents together, and it's easy to see Jake in them. His parents are holding each other and smiling at the camera. You can feel how much they love each other, though they are a bit of an odd couple. They are both incredibly fit, and war veterans, but she is much taller than his dad.

"She looks like a Viking," I say admiringly.

"She probably is one," he replies ruefully. "Anyway, enough pictures. I have something for you." He sounds excited. He takes my hand and leads me past the kitchen and the dining room and up a flight of stairs.

He brings me to his bedroom. On his bedside table is a huge leather-bound book with the words THE CHRON-

ICLES OF LUCITOPIA embossed on the bejeweled front cover.

"Have you read the whole book?" I ask him, reaching for it.

"Of course," he says, confused. "You haven't?"

"No," I admit sheepishly. I touch the cover with my hands. "Wait," I say, stepping back. "You knew how our story would end?"

"Almost?" he says like he's trying to remember a dream. "There are so many stories. And they're always changing." He frowns as he thinks about it. "I knew parts of it."

"Me too!" I say. "But I never knew all the details."

He smiles, nodding. "It was the same for me."

I look at the book. "Are we in there now?"

"No," he says. "Our story is locked. I think other people might be able to read it, but I couldn't find us in there anymore."

I look at him, and I can't seem to stop. This could become a habit.

He shakes himself and reaches under his pillow. He pulls something out and holds it behind his back.

"Is that for me?" I ask, grinning. I move closer to him.

"It's yours. I promised I would guard it, though I *thought* about taking it many times," he admits.

He pulls his hand out from behind his back and holds out my maiden's circlet.

I can't breathe. I touch my forehead where it used to rest. I wore it for a year. I don't know what to say.

"Here," Jake whispers, and he puts it back on my brow.

His hands run down either side of my face, then my throat, then he's pulling me to him and he's kissing me.

The falling, floating, flying feeling has nothing to do with an interdimensional shift this time. It's all Jake.

"A-hem."

We jump apart. Jake's dad is standing in the doorway in a t-shirt and sweatpants. I don't know how we woke him, seeing as how we were whispering. He must have a chastity detector in his brain. I hastily take off my maiden's circlet and hide it behind my back.

"Jake. No girls in your bedroom," his dad says gently, and a little disappointed, actually.

"We'll be right out," Jake says. He holds my hand tightly in his as he brings me to the door. He glances back at me. "I was just giving something back to her. For now."

Embarrassed but cheeky. Absolutely devastating.

"Will you stay for dinner?" Jake asks as we go down the stairs.

I frown. "I want to, but I can't."

He stops even though we're not all the way down yet. I'm one stair over him which puts us almost eye to eye. "Why not?" He's serious and a little worried. Like maybe things are different between us now that we're back here. He's frigging adorable. I know there are a lot of things he and I are going to have to learn about each other, but even if the whole world changes around us (like it just did) I'd still feel this way about him.

"I have a very important quest," I reply, breaking into a smile.

"Tell me your quest, Princess, and I will aid you in it," he says. His smile is so close to mine our lips are nearly touching.

"Okay," I say, shrugging. "But he bites."

ALSO BY JOSEPHINE ANGELINI

THE CHRONICLES OF LUCITOPIA

The Tinker's Daughter

Ensorcelled

STARCROSSED SERIES

Starcrossed

Dreamless

Goddess

Scions

Timeless

Outcasts

Endless

WORLDWALKER SERIES

Trial by Fire

Firewalker

Witch's Pyre

THRILLER

What She Found in the Woods

For more information please visit:

josephineangelini.com

Printed in the USA
CPSIA information can be obtained
at www.ICGtesting.com
JSHW021457280524
63780JS00004B/4

9 798987 832127